AWAKEN the DURGA WITHIN

Usha Narayanan is a gold medallist with a master's degree in English literature. She had a successful career in advertising, media and the corporate world before becoming a full-time author. A celebrated, skilful storyteller of mythological fiction, she has written *Pradyumna: Son of Krishna*, *The Secret of God's Son*, *Prem Purana: Mythological Love Stories* and *Kartikeya and His Battle with the Soul Stealer*. Her novels cut across genres and include a thriller and two romances. When she is not travelling or writing, Usha reads everything from thrillers to the puranas.

To know more about her, visit www.ushanarayanan.com or email her at author@ushanarayanan.com. Connect with her on www.facebook.com/writerusha or tweet @writerusha.

AWAKEN the DURGA WITHIN

FROM GLUM TO GLAM
CAGED TO CAREFREE

USHA NARAYANAN

RUPA

Published by
Rupa Publications India Pvt. Ltd 2018
7/16, Ansari Road, Daryaganj
New Delhi 110002

Sales Centres:
Allahabad Bengaluru Chennai
Hyderabad Jaipur Kathmandu
Kolkata Mumbai

Copyright © Usha Narayanan 2018

The views and opinions expressed in this book are the author's own
and the facts are as reported by her which have been verified to the extent
possible, and the publishers are not in any way liable for the same.

All rights reserved.
No part of this publication may be reproduced, transmitted,
or stored in a retrieval system, in any form or by any means,
electronic, mechanical, photocopying, recording or otherwise,
without the prior permission of the publisher.

ISBN: 978-93-5304-766-5

First impression 2018

10 9 8 7 6 5 4 3 2 1

Printed at Nutech Print Services, New Delhi

This book is sold subject to the condition that it shall not,
by way of trade or otherwise, be lent, resold, hired out, or otherwise
circulated, without the publisher's prior consent, in any form of binding or
cover other than that in which it is published.

For my mother,
who helped me slay my dragons.

Contents

Introduction:
Everything You Want to Be

'How can I say "no"? What will they think of me?'
'I'm scared. He's my boss and I can't tell him what I think!'

'My husband and children don't respect me. I don't know what to do!'

'I don't want to get married now, but my parents won't listen!'

Maybe you have said one of these things or wanted to say it out loud but were afraid to. Maybe you had no one to confide in, or found no one who would be non-judgemental and support you without question.

Well, here's a handy book, easy to read and follow, to help you be assertive and reclaim your life. Find practical solutions and principles you can begin to implement at once, proceeding at a pace that you are comfortable with. If you do not need this yourself, perhaps this is a book you can gift to someone you love: your mom, sister, daughter or friend.

Sounds interesting? Read on, then.

RECLAIMING YOUR VOICE

Like most women, you too probably hold back from doing something or asking for something because you feel diffident. You may wish to do something as simple as cutting your hair or trying out a new look. You may want to look for a job or join a course. If you are a working woman, perhaps you aspire for the senior post that is falling vacant soon. But you say nothing and do nothing to make this happen because you are afraid of what your mother, husband, boss or even your children will say. They will probably say that you are too old or young, or not good enough to do what you want. They may snuff out your dream in a moment, saying that your relatives or neighbours will disapprove—or worse still, they will laugh at you.

Your wish may be simply to have some fun—for example, you want to go on a trip to Dubai or Dehradun, but no one in your family wants to go with you. They have their own choices, ideas and friends. You may suggest that you could go with friends or with a women's group, but they do not want to let you do this either. They may believe that it is your job to cater to their needs and be available to cook, clean and keep the home running smoothly. If you go away for even a weekend, who will make their favourite pulao or pasta the way they like?

Perhaps you are a youngster, who's just about to begin college, and want your own vehicle—maybe one of those zippy scooters. It will make your life so much easier. You need not suffer creeps on the bus, who paw you or brush against you. You can attend as many maths classes as required to improve your scores. Maybe you can hang out occasionally at that new mall with your friends. You promise your parents that you will follow the road rules and wear a helmet. But they will not hear of it, giving a host of reasons to turn down your request. They say that it is too dangerous or that it will make it difficult to monitor your activities. Or they'll say that you will get a tan and then no one will marry you. Perhaps they go to the extent of saying, 'You already have a dusky complexion and all the fairness creams we got you are not helping.' You want to ask why it is okay for your brother to ride a bike even though he has fallen down a couple of times already. But what is the use? They will insist that a girl needs to be protected by her parents until they hand over that 'responsibility' to her husband.

Do any of these scenarios seem familiar? You can probably give me many such instances when you were denied a reasonable request, mainly because of your gender. Women all over the world—especially in India, where patriarchal traditions prevail—are often disregarded and their rightful needs ignored. The ideal girl, you are told, is one who obeys her parents during childhood, her husband during adulthood and her children when she is old. Perhaps you thought that being educated or even being employed would change your status. Sorry, that's not the deal! A well-brought-up girl is expected to sublimate her own desires for the sake of her family. Eat last, sleep last and sacrifice your desires in order to ensure the comfort of others. Emulate goddesses like Sita, who walked through fire, or Savitri, who followed her husband to Yamaloka.

Does this sound far-fetched? Not really. Just look at the news stories every day. You hear of honour killings, where a girl is punished for choosing a groom unacceptable to her parents or community, and of suicides committed by educated, well-employed women who face abuse at home. Occasionally, a woman complains of sexual harassment at work and then more skeletons tumble out, with others whispering about the abuse they faced and were too scared to come out with.

Ultimately, you find that, as a woman, you are forced to confront several issues that overwhelm you and prevent you from achieving your due. Whether you are a teenager, college-goer, working woman or stay-at-home mom, this book is for you. You will find within these pages, several pointers to help you balance your life and make it more meaningful and enjoyable. Discover what is preventing you from claiming your space. Find out how to change your behaviour so that you gain respect at home and success at work. Make choices that are right for you, not ones that others force on you. Choose to be yourself first, before being a mother, wife, employee, or whatever role you find yourself playing.

This is the true spirit of feminism, when women are given the same rights, power and opportunities as men and are treated in the same way as them. However, this does not mean that you should behave in a reckless, irresponsible manner (like some men do). Instead, choose freedom couched in responsibility, and liberation blended with wisdom.

DO YOU REALLY NEED THIS BOOK?

Perhaps you think that you do not need a book like this. Maybe your life is not so bad that it needs to be altered radically. But if you are browsing through this book, it means that you have felt a need for change. Maybe you feel uneasy about your life or think that you are missing something—a deeper purpose or direction. Some of you may already be facing a dire situation and are looking for help. You have dodged the issue too long by saying, 'What can I do? I do not have any money or a job. I am too timid to start a fight. I have to listen to what they say.' The mere thought of speaking up makes you breathe faster and your heart pound in fear. You may even be thinking that it is easy for a third person like me to say, 'Speak up for yourself!' when I have no idea of your specific circumstances.

But how long can you continue to suffer? You are growing more and more restless, angry or resentful. You are anxious all the time. It is beginning to affect how you eat, sleep, and eventually, your overall health. You think that there is no escape—that you are condemned to suffer for the rest of your days like many other women you know. There are a few lucky souls, no doubt, who enjoy fabulous careers, tons of money and an adoring husband. But life is always unfair. What can you do? Everything sounds pretty bleak. Is this the state in which you want to continue?

'I have spoken up a few times,' you may say. You may have protested when your boss or mother-in-law humiliated you in front of others: 'Your work is terrible', 'The house is like a pigsty', 'You have not brought up your kids properly'.

Sometimes the abuse is even more personal. 'You look like a slob,' or, 'You have no knowledge about finances. I am the one who earns and I will decide how my money is spent!' says your husband. Others in your family may support him, adding to your distress. How do you deal with it? You know you must protest, but often do not. You tell yourself that the abuse does not matter, but it does. 'What is the point of objecting when it won't change things?' you think. 'I might as well keep quiet.'

Is that the best or most sensible response? You know that the answer is 'NO'. You cannot retreat into a shell. Your trauma, if ignored, is likely to get worse. You may become increasingly bitter, beginning to think that no one loves or appreciates you, and no one really cares whether you live or die.

HOW THIS BOOK CAN HELP YOU

Maybe you are thinking: 'Well, my life is not so bad.' But are you sure of the future? Is it sensible to wait to learn swimming until you have fallen overboard, or to start exercising after you get a heart attack? If your marriage is in trouble, isn't it better to work on it now, rather than delay until your partner files for divorce?

The strategies offered in this book are not a last resort when you have hit rock bottom. Rather, they are habits you create and changes you implement right now so that you can lead a fruitful life. However, here's a word of caution: Women who are in a violent relationship may require more specialized help than a book can provide.

You can choose to read the chapters in any order,

depending on your own situation. The introduction, for instance, gives you examples of situations where your wishes are disregarded and highlights the need to change this pattern. The next one, 'What's Holding You Back?', focuses on the fears that prevent you from achieving success or peace of mind. The chapter titled, 'The Three Cs', introduces a three-step process that can set you free. 'A Homemaker Is Not a Slave' talks of ways in which a homemaker and/or mom can retain her self-respect and self-esteem. 'A Working Woman, Not a Pushover' delves into the many problems women face at the workplace and while balancing home and career. The next one, 'Young, Not Oppressed', deals with young women struggling to find their voice in personal or professional spheres. Finally, 'Reclaim Yourself and Your World' sums up the rewards of being assertive, not just to women but also to men and the community at large.

I have brought together my learnings, gleaned over several years of experience and observation as a housewife, a working woman holding responsible positions during a thriving career in advertising and media, and finally, as a successful author. I hope my book will inspire you to seek out a life of respect and dignity, and the right to speak up for what you feel and what you desire. I hope it will help free you from the rut you find yourself in, and start you off on your journey of self-discovery. This book provides you with tips, strategies and stories that will help you own your dream. I think of this book as my way of speaking up to help other women attain a rewarding life of their own.

A BONUS—FROM OUR MYTHOLOGY

When a woman is put down as being a subordinate being and someone who has no right to think for herself, zealots tell us that this is how it has always been in our society and that our scriptures condone this behaviour. They say that it is our cultural norm to worship the husband as 'god' and obey him, even when we know that he is making a mistake. But think about it: Even by their logic, if a husband is a god, does it not make the wife a goddess?

In Hindu mythology, a goddess or Devi is highly revered. She has many forms, like Durga, Lakshmi or Parvati. We offer her flowers and fruits, bring to her our problems, and pray for her help and guidance. Are these goddesses inferior to the gods? The answer is a resounding 'no'.

I read our ancient literature extensively while writing my mythology-based books—*Pradyumna: Son of Krishna, The Secret of God's Son, Prem Purana* and *Kartikeya and His Battle with the Soul Stealer*, wanting to find out the truth behind these claims. After all, my heroine Mayavati, in the first two books, is perhaps stronger and more committed to the right path than her husband is. And in *Prem Purana*, whether it is Mandodari standing her ground before Ravana, or Ganesha's three delightful wives making him work hard to win their hand in marriage, or Damayanti using her ingenuity to show Nala the right course of action, my characters always demonstrate the equality of the sexes. It is my firm belief that each individual must be given their due, based on their potential, and not on their gender. Do our religious texts—our puranas—support women or belittle them? When we say that we regard our women as goddesses, is that just one more way of imposing patriarchy? Let us find out in this book.

CAN A GODDESS BE WEAK?

When people say that a woman is a goddess, are they emphasizing her sex, indicating that as a female, she is inferior to her male counterpart? Well, the value placed on women has varied widely over time, as society and religion have always been ambivalent to feminine power.

The goddess is worshipped as 'Shakti', or the cosmic energy, without whom Shiva cannot function. She is regarded as Prakriti (nature) and also as Maya (illusion). Based on her actions, she is regarded as creative or destructive, benevolent or terrible, liberating or binding. A goddess, and by extension a woman too, can grant salvation, or tempt a man away from his path and impede his success. When she does the former, she is to be worshipped and when she does the latter, she is to be shunned as being dangerous. Man is seen as a representative of order and culture, and woman as a symbol of chaos and untamed nature. Her sexuality and freedom must be curbed by marriage and child-rearing duties for the safety of men and society at large. So, a woman is literally bound with rings on her fingers and toes, and with waistbands and necklaces, and asked to tie up her hair so as not to tempt men into lust! Her energy and love must be transferred to her husband, and thereby, controlled. This applies to goddesses as well: The domesticated Gauri, holding Ganesha in her lap, is the ideal to be worshipped; blood-drinking Kali, her hair unbound, roaming unrestrained and unclothed, is to be feared and considered dangerous.

However, folk traditions and rural India have a rich tradition of goddess-worship, which precedes the worship of male gods. The deities worshipped were called Amman, Amba or Mata, and were represented by natural features such as trees, huge rocks or anthills, indicating their closeness to the natural world. The goddess was an Earth Mother, who embodied both destructive and protective powers, and women sought her help to fight a society that attempted to control and exploit them.

Even our epics have extolled fiery heroines such as Draupadi, who is central to the epic *Mahabharata*. She is dragged into the Kuru court and one of the princes begins to disrobe her in order to humiliate her. She pleads with her husbands, the Pandavas, to help her, and when they remain silent, she raises her voice in defiance and escapes dishonour by virtue of her devotion to Krishna. Draupadi inspires women even today, as they see in her vulnerability a reflection of their own plight to survive exploitation. Her rage serves as a rallying point to continue their own fight against injustice and abuse.

Shakti herself is portrayed in the *Devi Purana* as the first and foremost of deities, and it is she who creates Brahma, Vishnu and Shiva, instructing them to create, preserve and destroy the universe. She promises to divide herself into three parts and become wives to the three of them. However, Shiva wants her for himself and plunges into ardent penances to win her. The other two try to win her too, but when she takes a terrifying form in order to test them, Brahma becomes four-faced as he turns away from her and Vishnu closes his eyes and plunges into the water. Only Shiva remains unperturbed and continues his penance. Shakti then promises him that she would be born as Sati and marry him.

This is quite a contrast to other stories featuring Parvati praying endlessly to marry Shiva, isn't it? So you can see that our ancient lore offers examples of the goddess being revered even more than the god. As our society evolves, more options and roles are opening up for women. We need to choose the right role models and interpret the stories of the goddesses in ways that are more empowering. In this way, we can choose to stand up for what we believe in—whether it is for our loved ones, women, community, animals, or our own fulfilment.

LESSONS WE LEARN FROM SHAKTI

Perhaps you are wondering how Parvati's story is relevant to you. Let us assume that you have a demanding software job and that someday you hope to start your own company. You are dating a man who is caring and successful, but also rather settled in his habits and used to doing things his own way. Maybe you are assertive at your workplace and manage a team, but when it comes to your romantic relationship, you end up falling in line with his wishes and then losing your cool when resentment builds up. How do you play the many roles you need to play, and harmonize your needs with his? You are afraid of becoming a pushover like your mother, who says, 'Ask your father!' for everything. But at the same time you do not want to be fighting all the time. How do you find the right balance between being soft and strong?

Who else can teach you this better than Parvati? Bring to mind her different forms depicted in pictures and carvings.

In one, she is dancing, while in another, she is embracing her husband. In yet another, she is Durga on her lion, killing the demon who threatens the world. She is also a yogini, meditating on the Ultimate. She is Kamini, the lustful goddess enchanting Shiva. She is the teacher and the student; she is the fond daughter and loving mother. Parvati is the cosmic power of the universe and an equal partner in her marriage. And when you meditate on her, she transforms your consciousness, allowing you to expand your spirit beyond your personal and social limitations so that you may imbibe her divine qualities.

You go to a movie or concert and come back walking like the heroine, pretending that you are singing like her, don't you? Imagine, how much greater is the power of a Devi, where the word itself means 'the shining one'. Her energy transforms your mind, allowing you to make changes that expand the possibilities in your physical life. Like the Devi, you too have multiple arms with which you multitask, keeping ahead of your duties and the demands placed on you. You liberate qualities within yourself that reflect those of the goddesses—Lakshmi's bountiful power, Saraswati's creative inspiration and Durga's warrior-like energy.

I hope that the following stories of various goddesses will enlighten and inspire you, helping you invoke the Shakti within you. For, she resides in you and in every woman who is struggling to find her place in the world. She will bring you power and prosperity. All that she asks you to do is to begin your journey with her—TODAY!

Let us start this process of liberating you with a story of Durga, the slayer of Mahishasura.

Free the Durga within You

The boundless power of Shakti incarnated in the universe as Durga, in order to counter the asura Mahisha. The demon had sought the boon of immortality from Brahma after performing a fierce tapasya for 10,000 years. But when the Creator said that he could not grant anyone this wish, the asura replied, 'Let my death not come by the hand of man, deva, or by the powers of the Trimurti—Brahma, Vishnu and Shiva. Let death come to me only through a woman.' He thought that women were weak and powerless and would not be able to kill him. Hence, he would be as good as immortal. Brahma smiled a secret smile and granted him his boon. Mahisha, who was half human and half buffalo, proclaimed his elation with a resounding bellow, tossing his head with its huge curved horns and flicking his immense tail. He then went on a rampage with his savage demon commanders, decimating the armies of mighty kings to become the overlord of the earth.

Emboldened by his successes, Mahisha planned an attack on the devas, envious of the powers they wielded from the heavens. He performed a grand sacrifice under the guidance of his guru Shukra and then advanced towards Amaravati, the capital of the celestial king, Indra. The gods of thunder and fire, and of water and wind, met with their guru Brihaspati and pondered over the challenge issued by Mahisha to surrender or face death at his hands. How could the great gods surrender to the asura, that too without a fight? Indra sent back a brash message, saying, 'I will slay you, buffalo! And I will make myself a bow with your horn.'

The devas confronted Mahisha on the battlefield, only to find that Brahma's boon made the asura impervious to their weapons. He could not be killed by Indra's thunderbolt, by Yama's noose or Agni's fire. They then sought refuge in the Trimurti. Vishnu came to the battlefield and tried to kill him with his luminous Sudarshana Chakra. But the discus was also rendered powerless and Vishnu retreated from the battle, along with Shiva and Brahma. The deva army fled and the asuras entered Amaravati with roars of triumph, seizing its treasures and capturing the divine dancers to make them dance for their pleasure.

The devas prayed ceaselessly to Vishnu to restore their powers to them while the earth trembled, and life withered under the cruel asura rule. 'Only a Devi can kill Mahisha,' said Vishnu. 'So let us combine our powers to create a woman who can kill him.'

At once, a dazzling red fire emerged from Brahma's face and stood burning before them. A pillar of light blazed forth from Shiva's brow, glittering like silver. From Vishnu flowed his power, in the form of a blue flame. The three forces combined to create an incandescent light into which merged the powers of Indra, Yama, Agni and the other devas. From this brilliance was formed a beautiful yet fearsome woman, who was tall as the sky and had eighteen arms. Her face was formed from Shiva's power, her eyes from Agni and her arms from Vishnu. The gods gave her their weapons too—Vishnu's chakra, Shiva's trident, Varuna's war conch, Yama's staff of death, Indra's thunderbolt, and Vayu's bow and quiver with unending arrows. They worshipped her as Devi, Bhagavati, and Durga—the Invincible One. 'You are the creator of heaven and earth, the preserver of virtue and life, the destroyer of disease and death. Bend your mighty bow, divine Mother, and save us from Mahisha who can be slain only by you.'

Durga raised her hand in blessing and they trembled in bliss. She laughed a terrible laugh and the mountains quaked in fear. Then she mounted her magnificent lion to ride towards Amaravati. Mahisha heard her dreadful roar that far surpassed that of any beast, and grew angry. 'Go find out who dares laugh so loudly outside our gates,' he said to his soldiers. His men saw the magnificent goddess advancing on the rampaging lion and ran back in fear to tell their king about the radiant woman riding on a golden lion.

Mahisha was filled with lust on hearing of this extraordinary woman and sent his minister to her, with a small army, to speak on his behalf. 'Praise the woman's beauty with extravagant words. Tell her that the mighty Mahisha, Lord of the Worlds, seeks to marry her. Then bring her to me without harming her splendour, for I wish to enjoy her loveliness in my bed!' he said.

The minister approached the Devi, trembling, and told her, 'Lustrous One! Who are you and from where have you come? My king, the great Mahisha, blessed by Brahma, invincible on earth and heaven, wishes you to adorn his court with your beauty. Come with us to be his queen and he will shower you with rare gems and grant you everything you desire.'

The goddess laughed at him and her lion roared. 'Tell your king that I am Durga, who embodies all the powers of the gods. No god is invincible before my powers, least of all an asura,' she said, her voice like thunder. 'How dare a monster and a beast like your king aspire to my hand? I could burn you to ashes in an instant for your impudence, but I restrain myself knowing that you are merely following orders. Tell your arrogant king that I am born not to wed him but to kill him.'

'But how can you kill anyone, when you do not even have an army?' persisted the minister. 'O Devi, you are delicate and desirable, while my master is dreadful and daunting. He will crush you in an instant like an elephant trampling a garland of flowers.'

'You are a fool serving a bigger fool if you think that Mahisha's army or his fortress will save him,' she replied. 'Both of you seem to have forgotten that Mahisha is destined to be killed by a woman. I am the one born to bring about his doom, but will spare him if he will surrender Indra's throne and retreat to the netherworld. If he does not, I will dispatch him there myself, with or without an army.'

Her lion pawed the ground and lashed its tail impatiently, eager to attack. Still the minister persisted with his plea, hoping to complete the task assigned to him. 'Discard your bravado, wondrous Durga!' he said.

'There is no need for you to lie and posture like other women do. Remember that a woman is created solely for a man's pleasure. My soldiers have been restrained thus far only because our king has ordered us to be gentle. Do not test our patience further, and come with us. Thank your destiny for it has brought you a glorious future to enjoy the treasures of earth and heaven as Mahisha's queen.'

Durga roared in response and the minister's horse attempted to bolt in fear. The minister struggled to control his mount and screamed in terror when the lion clawed at him with one raised foot. He abandoned his quest and fled to his king to tell him everything that had happened. However, arrogant Mahisha sneered at his fear and her challenge. He ordered his fearsome generals to subdue her through their warcraft and occult skills and bring her to him without harming her beauty.

The generals went before her and gazed, awestruck, at her breathtaking radiance and the fierce weapons in her many hands. One of them finally gathered his wits together in order to try and coax her to accept Mahisha's suit. 'No woman would turn down a proposal from the sovereign of the three realms. Maybe you do so because you are overwhelmed by Mahisha's fame and power or due to a maiden's natural bashfulness. Or is it that you are devious like all women and wish to use your wiles to increase my king's desire? Know that Mahisha is already inflamed with lust for you and abandon your pretence. If you do not submit now, you will regret your obstinacy.'

'Stop, fool!' she roared in reply. 'Why would I marry a buffalo when I am wedded to the great god Mahadeva, the One without beginning or end, who is omnipresent and omniscient? Do you not understand that a woman is neither a weakling nor an object of lust? Tell your king that I will dispatch him to Yama, who rides a buffalo, to become the god's second mount.' She raised her dreadful axe threateningly and the generals retreated, confused over what to do next, for they needed their king's permission to take her by force.

Mahisha asked his ministers and generals for their counsel. Ugly Durmukha, master of occult powers, told Mahisha, 'How strong can a woman be, my king? So what if she has eighteen arms or a thousand? I will slice them off and her head, too, if you order me to. When I have the power to kill Yama, Indra and Agni, the fiercest of gods, what threat can a mere woman pose? Perhaps you are diffident because Brahma's boon renders you vulnerable to a woman. But nothing can hold me back except your command. Grant me permission now and I will sally forth to subdue her and drag her before you to use as you please. Let us end this endless debate over a trivial matter.'

Not to be outdone, another general sought to please the king with flattery. 'The woman's fierce words are merely an attempt to increase your passion, great Mahisha!' he said. 'When she says "no", she means "yes". When she asks you to go away, she means just the opposite—that she desires you. If she says she will kill you, she merely means that she will slay you with her lush body and coy glances. Her promise to take your life merely indicates that she will bear your children. Send her rich gems, silks and perfumes, and I assure you she will yield.'

The minister who had gone as a messenger to Durga spoke up in a quivering voice. 'I have had dreadful dreams through the night, O king,' he said. 'I saw your men marching headless into Yama's dark domain. Now I see bats and owls gathering in dark clouds overhead, though day has dawned. We should heed these dreadful omens that foretell danger.'

For a moment, Mahisha felt a deep unease, as if his death was calling him. But then, bloodthirsty Durmukha spoke up again. 'Should we withdraw now because the minister speaks in fear like an old woman? Can anyone take down your dreaded asuras who vanquished Indra and his devas? Our glory is at stake and we must fight, or the world will scoff at us for running away from a mere woman! '

Roused by his words, the other asuras also clamoured for war and Mahisha sent them out to tame the brash challenger. They attacked Durga with swords and clubs but she sent them flying with the flaming weapons she wielded in her eighteen arms. The fierce commanders met their death, one by one, bludgeoned by her mace and impaled by her trident. More demons streamed out of Mahisha's fortress like a river of death. Durga conjured up a chariot from which she fought, while her lion expanded its form and swallowed her foes whole or tore off their heads, leaving a crimson trail in his wake. Durmukha used his mace to land a fearsome blow on the lion, which so enraged Durga that she flew at him and beheaded him with her battle axe. Her arrows flew forth like a glittering wave, destroying the asuras by the thousands. Her arms were a blur as she used chakra and trident, mace and spear, to unleash a river of blood on which floated the severed heads of the asuras. The heavenly musicians sang songs praising the great goddess and the devas showered a gentle rain of flowers on her, hailing her victory.

Mahisha came forth himself to confront her but grew weak with desire when he set eyes on her luminous beauty. He changed his form into that of a handsome man, dressed in opulent silks and jewels, in order to woo her. His arrogance made him believe that no one could resist his might and splendour. 'O Durga! Your eyes slay me as your arrows never may!' he said. 'Your curved body defeats me as your scimitar can never hope to do. The great Mahisha, lord of heaven and earth, bows his proud head to you as he never has before. Grant me a glimpse of your beauty, not your bravado. Accept me as your lover and return with me to spend your days in my arms in ceaseless pleasure.'

Durga magnified her form before his astonished eyes and uttered a final warning. 'Foolish asura, forsake your lust and open your senses to the ultimate truth. Know that you stand before Shakti, who creates and destroys the universe at will. I have taken up this form only to destroy evil and restore dharma—the path of righteousness. When I am the embodiment of eternal bliss, why would I be attracted by your offer of sensual pleasure? When I am married to the great Shiva, the Transcendent One, why would I take a beast for my lover? If you wish to live, submit to me, restore the heavens to the devas and retreat to the netherworld. Or face me in battle and die!' She blew such a blast on her war conch and twanged her bow so loudly that it seemed as if the skies would crack from the sound.

The asura was enraged by her scornful words and his eyes burned scarlet. 'You have shown that you are only an ignorant woman by turning me down, Devi!' he roared. 'You forget that you speak to the invincible Mahishasura, who made the Trimurti flee in fear. I will make you suffer. I will make you pay a terrible price for your harsh words.'

Durga looked at the king ranting, and seeing that his ego prevented him from seeing the truth, she laughed a scornful laugh that echoed up to the heavens. Her derision, more than her words, cut the asura to the quick and he finally realized that she meant what she said. This hateful woman had killed his brave generals, his loyal soldiers and now stood mocking him. His wrath transformed him back to his beastly form and he tossed his head with its sharp horns and pawed the ground with his cloven hooves. He took up his bow and engulfed her in a torrent of arrows. But the goddess sent forth her own arrows that destroyed them and broke his bow as well. The asura took up a lion's form and gouged her lion with his claws. Durga's lion roared in challenge and slashed at his chest to tear out his heart. Mahisha then changed himself into a gigantic elephant and charged forward, hurling huge rocks at Durga. However, her lion tore into him while she herself hurled her formidable mace at his head. Defiant still, Mahisha turned into a giant serpent and sprang forward with a fierce hiss, his poisonous fangs bared. But Durga's giant sword hacked into his neck, forcing him to abandon this form and return to his buffalo form. He lashed out with his hooves, his tail swishing in anger, uttering a fierce bellow that threatened the skies.

Growing tired of his belligerence, Durga sent forth her glittering Sudarshana Chakra. The dauntless weapon sliced off Mahisha's head from his body. The head fell to the ground with a thud and his body followed—a mountain from which flowed rivers of blood. The surviving asuras saw their leader fall and fled, howling, chased by the Devi's lion. The devas rejoiced and appeared before her to worship her and extol her valour. The invincible Mahisha had been destroyed by the glorious Shakti, the mother of the universe, and the world was at peace again.

WHAT DURGA TEACHES YOU

Do you see several echoes from your own life in what the Devi faced? She too is seen as an object of lust, and as someone who is foolish and inferior to males. Her objections and protests against pursuit and persecution are dismissed as an attempt to increase male lust. She counters all this resolutely, reinforcing the message, 'no means no', which was recently highlighted in the movie, *Pink*.

What can you learn from Durga? You see her here as someone who embodies all the powers of the male gods. Some puranas even depict her as the Supreme One, who created the Trimurti and the world. The more she is harassed, the more aggressive she becomes. Her eighteen arms represent the multifaceted ability of a woman to play many roles to sustain and protect her family, society and the universe at large. The Devi's killing of Mahisha represents a woman's courage in standing up for herself against the evils surrounding her.

Do these actions make her brutal and bloodthirsty? Are you afraid that being bold like her will make you unpleasant or unpopular? Look upon Durga's face and you will find her smiling as she calmly goes about cleansing the world, a task that needs to be done. She is not cruel, nor eager to destroy. She is in fact transforming the world for the better, showing you how you can do that too. She summons you, her daughter, to join the fight against the injustice and humiliation that you often face. She tells you that you can take control of your life and change prevailing conditions. You can put a stop to the exploitation and manipulation and free yourself from the pain and suffering. Not just for yourself, you must also be equipped to protect your loved ones—daughters, sisters, the young, the old and helpless animals. To do this, you must take the initiative and protest vehemently against violence, working towards creating a purer world.

The *Mahabharata* shows us how Draupadi challenges her tormentors and their very concept of dharma, when faced with a crisis that will make most women collapse in tears. She questions, prods and forces the Kuru king to placate her with a boon. She uses this boon to win back freedom but finds herself standing alone at the end of the Kurukshetra war, which destroys her people and her sons. But even her loss does not weaken her spirit and she persuades her husband, Yudhishthira, to ascend the throne and establish righteousness again.

From this gallant princess and other epic heroines like her, you learn that a woman's nurturing instincts should not limit her to the domestic sphere. Like Draupadi, you need to challenge conventional thinking that portrays women as having no voice in their own lives, as being 'possessions' that can be shared or pledged, or as objects of lust. Draupadi is far wiser than all the other characters of the epic, with the exception of Krishna. She knows what is right and makes her decision accordingly. She is a powerful symbol of womanhood and of the principle of equality in marriage and society.

You will meet other heroines in the following chapters who will guide and inspire you on your voyage of liberation. Let us start the journey now, shall we?

1
What's Holding You Back?

Before you answer that, let us talk about something totally different—lipstick! 'Why lipstick?', I can hear you thinking. Well, when do you use lipstick—when you are going out, when you want to put on your 'public' face, put your best foot forward, etc.? Perhaps you are looking for your Prince Charming, or you want to look your best on your first day in college. Choose the reason that fits your circumstances.

You have put on your best sari or outfit, and your hair is combed and fluffed out to frame your face. You dab on your favourite perfume and bring out the dressy sandals that you have saved for a special occasion. You use the lip liner and fill in that enchanting plum or pink or deep red lipstick that you adore. All this is like the warpaint that native Americans wear to stun or impress the world. Your make-up tells those who see you that you are ready to face any challenge that life may throw at you.

You may encounter your first hurdle at home itself, where someone objects to you wearing lipstick. 'No one in our family paints their face like this. You look stupid/cheap!' they say. What do you do? Is your first instinct to rush to your room to scrub off all the colour? Stop right there. Just smile with your freshly coloured lips and continue whatever you are doing. If you have time, find some place where you can sit and calmly think things through. If you live near a beach, go there whenever you can and watch the waves crashing again and again on the shore. Remind yourself that the water—or your critics—cannot touch you unless you allow it. If not a beach, find a neighbourhood park. Walk alongside other people and hear them talk. Sit on a bench under a tree. Listen to the birds. Breathe deeply. Watch the kids play. Enjoy the moment. Plan on how you will enjoy every moment of your life. And most importantly: Do not let your mother-in-law, your father or your supposed friend mess with your mind. What really matters is what you think, what you wish for. Look at the smiling woman walking by. Does she not have problems? Maybe her husband is not in favour of her taking time out to go for a walk. But here she is, knowing that she must take care of her well-being, both physical and mental.

Now, let us move on to discuss whatever is troubling you, and the fears that hold you back from achieving personal satisfaction. In the first place, are you sure that your fears are even real? Perhaps you are too diffident to even try changing your behaviour. You will often find that you are your own worst enemy when you let your inhibitions and habits keep you back. If you sail forth confidently, people may just step out of your way. You will not know unless you try it.

Try speaking up at home or at work, whichever is your personal battlefield, and wherever you feel anxious, afraid or suppressed. Maybe you will find that you face no opposition. You will then wonder why you never tried this before. Or you may find that your fears are true and that you do face obstacles. No worries even then! Keep reading and you will get there.

Let us find out what the hurdles are and how to remove them. Sometimes, you may just need to be patient and persistent. At other times, you may need to cut yourself off completely from something that is totally hopeless.

THIRTEEN ISSUES THAT HOLD YOU BACK

1. *Your first hurdle is that you are conditioned to accept what others say, without question.* You think that you have to follow instructions or assume that others know better than you. You never say 'no' as you do not even recognize this as an option. It is only later that you wonder if you could have refused. The fault does not lie with you, but with our culture that ties down a woman with several perverse notions. She is always expected to listen to elders, her husband, her in-laws, her son, her son-in-law—the list is endless.

2. *Another common reason for diffidence is that you want to be liked, rather than respected.* You want your neighbours, your relatives, even your milkman to think that you are nice. But what if the milkman is unreliable or your maid runs circles around you when you point out how many days she has absented herself? Are you going to take this lying down? Think about it.

3. ***Maybe you are afraid to draw attention to yourself by protesting***. You feel more comfortable being part of the crowd, taking your lead from others. You are afraid that if you voice a different opinion, others may shun you or throw you out of the group. You tell yourself, 'I am happy the way I am. I don't want to be called a loudmouth who is always arguing!' Really? Do you not have a right to voice an opinion? Wouldn't it be nice if someone listened to you at least sometimes? Should you not exercise your choice when it is important to you?

4. ***Perhaps you lack the self-confidence to stand up for yourself***. 'What if I make a mistake?' you wonder, and remain silent. But how do you learn unless you make mistakes? One of the indicators of intelligence is the ability to adapt to circumstances and learn from experience. You do not achieve anything by cowering in a corner and allowing life to pass you by.

5. ***Another reason why you may stay silent is that you are afraid that if you assert yourself, people will say that you have an 'attitude'***. 'When all of us agree, why is she acting smart?' they may say. So you hurry to say 'yes' as you don't want to be the odd one out. After all, you have to deal with them every day. Even as you read this, you may be thinking, 'I have to be accommodative. It's easy for someone to tell me that I should be fearless and contradict the popular view. But only I know my circumstances. This is not a fairy tale where the heroine makes bold moves and succeeds. This is my life!' Hmm…did you hear what you just said? This is *your* life. And you should be living it, not cringing in fear.

6. ***Maybe you do not wish to hurt others by voicing your opinion or your desires***. Dealing with your family is often the biggest hurdle as you respond emotionally to situations that involve them. Your patterns of behaviour are long established. You are a child listening to your parents or a new bride trying to fit into your new home. You fall into habits of submissive behaviour in your need to be loved. Later, when you want to change this, you are unable to make progress as you cannot handle their hurt or resistance. For example, you may want to tell your family that you are tired of hosting the Diwali party year after year and it is time someone else hosted it. But you are afraid of how they will react. Or perhaps you want to tell your son to help you with the chores but are afraid that he will interpret this to signify that you no longer love him. Does this mean that you should be a martyr for life?

7. ***Maybe you are used to complaining about your situation but never do anything to change it***. Do you think there's nothing wrong in that? Well, it's time you realize that no one likes a complainer. The people you complain to will soon start avoiding you. Or worse still, they will make fun of you. No one likes someone who cribs about the sacrifices she is making.

8. ***Sacrifice***. You give up your desires, and neglect your own interests and even necessities like food and sleep, in your eagerness to take care of others. You let yourself be treated like dirt, because you think it is your duty to compromise, as that is what is expected of a woman. However, what happens if you become sick or depressed when you make this behaviour a habit? The ones who you served hand and

foot will be the first to turn around and ask you why you did not take care of yourself. 'Did I tell you to neglect your health?' they may ask. 'Now you've become a burden for all of us.' Is this something you wish to deal with when you are already feeling low and helpless? No point in regretting your actions when it is too late to reverse the damage. You may be a nurturer by instinct and that is in no way a bad thing—except when it comes at the cost of your own well-being. Make a resolve, today, that you will live the life you want to live rather than the one that others want you to live.

9. *Perhaps you have become a clinging vine, dependent on someone else, most often a male, to take care of you*. What happens in the future if you find yourself forced to fend for yourself, due to circumstances or fate? What if your partner dies or leaves you? Are you going to look around desperately for another person to look after you? It might not be very easy to do that!

10. *Maybe your problem with standing up for yourself is most evident when you deal with an authority figure*. It may be your boss, your parents, or loved ones. You succumb to pressure and toe the line unquestioningly. You are afraid to lose your job or face conflict. Yes, many women share this fear. When in danger, the two options for survival are fight or flight. More often than not, you choose the latter. You avoid or postpone conflict until you are cornered and can run no more. Is this the position that you want to be in?

11. *Perhaps you are one of those who acts or protests only when you are cornered*. At that point, you are forced to retaliate

strongly, in anger and desperation. You insult the person opposing you, and fly off the handle. 'You never respected me,' you shout. 'You always treated me badly. Ten years ago, you let your mother stomp all over me.' The accusations and the resentment spill out in a flood and you are unable to stop. The bitterness is so shattering that it makes it impossible to come to any compromise. The words you spill are poisonous and the relationship is broken forever. You are left with no option but to quit—your relationship, your job, your friendship, or whatever else the circumstance.

12. *Another reason you do not protest is that you are afraid you will lose opportunities in the future.* 'If I say "no" today, will they ask me again to organize our club's annual day?' 'If I turn down this assignment, will my boss postpone the promotion I crave? Is it better that I suck it up and do the task, instead of turning it down? I'm sure I can summon up the time and energy to complete it, no matter what it costs me.'

13. *You are afraid of other people's reactions when you suddenly stop being a doormat or speak up against their diktats.* Of course, they are going to be shocked, angered or displeased. Who wants to lose a slave who faithfully carries out their orders, however difficult or distasteful they may be? But does that mean you are going to have a rope around your neck for the rest of your days? If they love you and care for you, they will appreciate your reasons for taking a stand. If they do not, are they worth pandering to anymore? Is it not worthwhile to find out who cares for you and who does not? The earlier the better; for then you have more room to manoeuvre.

YOU ARE NOT ALONE

That's quite a list, is it not? Going through the different scenarios, you would have realized that you are not the only one in this quandary. The woman sitting next to you in the theatre, the neighbour in the adjacent flat, the girl with the laptop who runs to catch the bus each morning—each of them has a tale to tell. One is afraid that her needs will not be met; another, that she is being exploited. Yet another woman wishes she could speak her mind at least once, instead of putting up with the problems in her life. Many women are battered mentally and physically because they continue to tolerate abuse, thereby compromising their peace of mind or self-respect. Then they beat themselves up, wishing that they had been proactive and not merely reactive—that they had stood up for what they believed in.

As a woman, you not only face hurdles imposed by others, you also face conflict from within yourself. As mentioned earlier, this is often due to culture and upbringing, lack of self-confidence, or pulling back when you should be pushing ahead. You have made it a habit to demand less from yourself and from others, prioritizing everyone's needs before your own. Though you need to counter both external and internal obstacles, it may be easier to confront your inner demons first. Why? Because they are under your control and you can start the process today—right now, in fact!

Well, you have already made a beginning by reading this book. As Estée Lauder, one of the richest self-made women in the world put it, 'I didn't get there by wishing for it or hoping for it, but by working for it.' Your fears are real; the emotions that overwhelm you when you think of making a change are real. At times, fear is healthy, for it keeps you safe. Your senses or intuition warn you that there is something suspicious or dangerous about a person or a situation. Heed the warning! Ensure that you are not taking unnecessary risks, perhaps to prove a point to someone else. You are initiating a change for your own well-being, not for others. Do not give yourself a hard time as there are others already doing that. But when you have really decided to do something about it, you can change. The solution may be different for you and for another woman with different needs. But you need to address your fears and aim for a meaningful life even if it means disappointing or upsetting someone else. Remember: Whatever you do, there will always be some people who will never accept or appreciate you. You just need to keep going until you are at peace with yourself.

To do this, you should start with small steps—perhaps slide into the water instead of diving in. You need to motivate yourself sufficiently as well. One way to do this is to visualize how you will feel when you speak up against someone who is being unfair to you. Imagine your colleague's shocked face when you tell him that you will appreciate it if he acknowledges your contribution to the project the next time. Or visualize your mother-in-law's expression when you stop her from criticizing you in front of relatives, by saying: 'I'm sure we don't want to bore them with stories of my shortcomings. I have so many stories to share too!' Well, you may never say this, but the idea will bring a smile to your face and make it seem worthwhile.

Motivate yourself by thinking of the times you succeeded,

instead of dwelling on failures. Failure is no big deal. You learned something, didn't you? And you will not be making the same mistake again. At least you tried something that not many others can boast of. Remind yourself of your talents— in singing, maths, chess. Do not let anyone make you feel that you are worthless. Also, do not overthink and come up with all sorts of ways in which things can go wrong. This will merely increase your fears and immobilize you. Instead, equip yourself to face challenges and use situations to make a change in your own character. You are not a rock that is meant to merely exist or endure. You are flesh and blood, and the world must honour your feelings and desires.

To summarize, there are many reasons why you are the way you are. Stop blaming yourself. Analyse your fears and know that there is a solution for every problem. You don't have to be the nice woman, the whiner, the clinging vine or the doormat. It's your life and you have a right to your opinions and your happiness. And here's a tip to encourage and reward you for coming this far!

> **Tip:** *The first rule for you to remember is to say 'no' when someone asks you to do something you do not wish to do. Remember that you have a right to choose. You often forget that, don't you? Saying 'no' can simplify your life so much—just try it! I will elaborate more about this later.*

Now, let's move on to a story that shows how Sati and her incarnation, Parvati, are models for a powerful woman, not for one who is subordinate to men and whose very existence hinges on her husband's. Let us see how Shiva acknowledges that he and Shakti are the same. In fact, Shivaa is the first of the 1,008 names by which the world worships her.

Who is Sati? According to popular belief, she is the model of the ideal wife who serves her husband faithfully while he lives, and burns herself on his pyre when he dies! This is not true, but merely a distorted belief. As Ravana's wife Mandodari puts it: 'A sati is one who follows dharma; not one who worships at her husband's feet and kills herself on his death.' Shall we revisit Sati's story then, looking at it from a different viewpoint, as written in our very own puranas?

Sati, Parvati and You

Ages ago, Brahma prayed to Shiva, seeking the power to create women so that man could unite with her and carry out his task of populating the world. Shiva, who was Ardhanarishwara, half male and half female, detached the great goddess Shakti from his body. Shakti sent forth her own power into the cosmos as Prakriti—the spirit of creation and the cause of all actions in the entire moving and unmoving universe. Her divine task was to be Shiva's beloved in every incarnation and to soften the ascetic god by bringing him into the world of householders. She would, thereby, fulfil the purpose of the created world. Shakti became real, or 'sat', and was born as Sati, the daughter of Brahma's son Daksha, who was an ardent devotee of Adi Parashakti. Shiva smiled at his beloved wife and together they played a celestial game, behaving like mortals in order to teach man how life was to be lived.

The divine Sati glowed with heavenly lustre when she was born and Daksha bowed his head in reverence to her. The goddess spoke to him thus: 'I will remain your daughter only as long as you give me respect. If you fail to do so at any time, I will cast off my body, return to my original self and then take another form.' Daksha nodded in acceptance and the child took on a mortal form. Blessed by her birth, the three realms were filled with bliss, beauty and fragrance. However, as years passed, Daksha gradually forgot that his daughter was not just his child but the Great Goddess herself, born as a result of his tapasya.

Sati was enchanting in her beauty and wise beyond her years. Her mind was fixed on the great three-eyed god who lived on the mystic, snow-topped mountain of Kailasa. Sati decided that she would attract Shiva by her asceticism. The devas in heaven, too, approached Shiva and asked him to take a wife. However, absorbed in his dhyana, Shiva refused their request, saying that marriage was a form of bondage and that he did not wish to be enmeshed in the travails of the world. However, when they entreated him further, he agreed to marry, as long as his bride could be a yogini when he was a yogi; and a kamini—a loving wife—when he felt passionate. The devas spoke to him of Sati, who had been performing severe austerities to attain him, and he agreed to marry her for the sake of his devotees.

A resplendent Shiva appeared before Sati—four-armed, three-eyed and five-faced—and blessed her with a boon. She was bashful and he was swift to grant her unspoken wish: 'Yes, you will be my wife,' he said. Charmed by her loveliness, the great yogi became an eager suitor and asked Daksha for her hand in marriage. When Daksha hesitated, Brahma commanded him to accept Shiva's request. The marriage took place in the presence of sages and devas. The ascetic Shiva wilfully entered the world of maya, and the couple retired to his mountain cave to sport in love.

Daksha was unhappy, however, as he thought that he deserved a wealthy son-in-law and not one who lived on cremation grounds, surrounded by ghouls and goblins. He performed a grand yagna to which he invited all the gods and sages, but excluded Shiva and Sati. Sati encountered Soma, the moon, on his way to the yagna with his wife Rohini, and came to Shiva to tell him that they should attend the yagna too. 'What respect can we gain by going uninvited?' protested Shiva, but she was adamant. 'You are the lord of sacrifices and to conduct one without inviting you is an insult to both of us. If you will not come, I will still go and rebuke my father for disregarding dharma,' she declared. He nodded in agreement and sent her with a retinue consisting of Nandi, his foremost devotee, and 60,000 of his attendants. Sati confronted Daksha and said, 'Father, why have you spurned your daughter and your son-in-law, who is the Supreme God and the very spirit of the yagna?'

'My yagna is sacred! I cannot invite a half-naked beggar whose lineage is unknown, who wears ashes and serpents and dances on graves!' roared Daksha.

'A man who abuses the great Shiva is my enemy!' said Sati, her eyes aflame. 'I am defiled by your profanity and unwilling to return to Kailasa. I no longer wish to live as your daughter when you show me and Shiva no respect, thereby disrespecting dharma. I will cast off this body and be born again to a righteous father whom I can honour and love.' Her wrath transformed her into her celestial form of Adi Parashakti. Seeing her in her fiery form, the devas present at the yagna trembled and Daksha's attendants scattered in terror. Her soul left her body, bringing destruction to those who had dishonoured her and Shiva.

In distant Kailasa, Shiva roared in rage as he discerned all that had happened. From his body were born the ferocious, eight-armed Virabhadra, and the dreadful, dark-hued Bhadrakali, who was Shakti's own dire incarnation. The two descended, howling, on the sacrificial grounds, destroying all who were present and plucking Daksha's head off his shoulders with their nails. Shiva's anger was now transformed to grief and he mourned the loss of his Sati, placing her body on his shoulders and dancing the tandava of death. His arms flailed the three realms and his hair swished around his head, scattering the stars. His feet thudded on the ground, causing the seas to spew flames and volcanic mountains to erupt with snow. The world shuddered— at the brink of annihilation—until Vishnu used his chakra to cut Sati's body into 108 pieces that fell on earth—in Kashi, Pushkar, Gaya, and other places that became Shakti Peethas, her divine abodes. Here, she would be worshipped in her many forms—as Sita in Chitrakoot, Rukmini in Dwaraka, Radha in Vrindavan, Vindhyavasini in the Vindhyas, Gayatri in Pushkar, and Mahalakshmi in Kolhapur.

Calm again after his tandava, merciful Shiva restored to life all those who had been slain—even the foolhardy Daksha, who was now given the head of a goat. Daksha and the devas sang praises of Shiva, who retired once again to his cave, to continue his dhyana.

Taking courage from his absence, the demon Tarakasura undertook a fierce penance seeking a boon from Brahma that he should be killed by no one except Shiva's son. He deemed it a near impossibility, for Shiva had forsworn marriage and the world, grieving the loss of his Sati. The world floundered in evil, with the devas deposed from their thrones, and Tarakasura rampaging across heaven and earth. The powerless Indra prayed to Adi Parashakti to incarnate again on earth so that her son with Shiva could put an end to the demon's havoc. 'Save us, O Devi, or Tarakasura will destroy the worlds,' they pleaded.

Peerless Shakti blessed them with a vision of her Vishvarupa, in which she embodied the universe. The realms of truth and bliss were her crown. The sun and moon were her eyes, and the Vedas— the sacred texts of the Hindu faith—her speech. All creations formed her body, which glowed with the brilliance of a thousand suns. The devas gazed at her in wonder and saw that they were present within her as well. She then transformed herself into a dire form with countless heads and faces, rolling eyes and a searing gaze. Galaxies exploded around her and flames surrounded her, blinding their eyes and confounding their senses. They cried out in fear and pleaded for mercy.

The Devi took pity on them and resumed her benevolent form, promising to protect them from Taraka. 'I will be born again on earth as Parvati, the daughter of Himavan,' she said, and disappeared into her lofty realm. Heavenly drums reverberated in joy and the demons had a premonition that death was near.

The daughter of the Himalayan mountain king, young Parvati was resolute in her focus on Shiva, for she knew well the purpose of her birth. Her father sought Shiva's permission to visit him every day with his daughter, in order to serve him. However, the god replied that he should come alone to his cave to serve him, and not bring Parvati. The young girl looked at him with luminous eyes and said, 'Perhaps you should consider who you are and who Prakriti is.'

'Why should I?' Shiva retorted. 'I do not need Nature. I will destroy her with my ascetic heat.'

'How is that possible?' the young girl argued. 'How can you live without Nature? The mountain you live in, the food you eat, the very air you breathe…everything is but an expression of Prakriti. You cannot exist without her, though you pretend not to know it. If you are indeed beyond Nature, then why avoid me? You have no reason to fear.'

Shiva admired her courage and clear wit and allowed her to stay. He was fascinated by her beauty and her intelligence, but still resisted falling in love. The desperate devas, suffering under Taraka, sent Kama to shoot his arrows of love at the three-eyed god. Afflicted by passion but still unwilling to accede to its power, Shiva burned Kama to ashes and returned again to his dhyana. Parvati would not accept defeat and consoled Kama's wife Rati, saying that she would evoke passion in Shiva's heart and bring Kama back to life. She began a fierce penance, standing amidst fierce fires in summer and icy waters in winter, offering her prayers to Shiva.

Her father attempted to dissuade her, telling her that it was impossible to attain Shiva. Her mother also pleaded with her to abandon her rigorous penance in the forest and return to the comforts of their palace. But Parvati could not be deterred. 'Shiva has shunned the comforts of home and hence I will not be able to gain his favour from our palace, mother,' she said. 'I shall bring him here, before me, and destroy the Rudratva—the dreadfulness of Rudra—with my penance.'

The heat of her tapasya scorched the heavens and the devas again entreated Shiva to marry her and beget a son to destroy Taraka. The compassionate Mahadeva, who had swallowed the poison that arose from the cosmic ocean in order to save the universe, agreed to help his devotees. But first, he would test Parvati's resolve by sending the seven sages to question her. The sages described Shiva in disparaging terms—as a hermit, a savage and as the embodiment of everything that is unholy. 'How can you bear to embrace a creature who wears skulls and hissing snakes around his neck? What happiness can you expect, living amidst burning pyres, ghosts and spirits?' they asked.

Parvati listened to them with respect and then told them that their perception of the great god was one-sided. She countered their arguments and spoke convincingly of Shiva's immeasurable glory. The sages smiled and went back to Kailasa to convey her resolve to the god with the matted locks. Shiva decided to go to Parvati himself, attracted both by her beauty and her resolve.

Taking the form of an old Brahmin, he advised her to turn her thoughts away from Shiva. 'Choose elegant Indra, charming Vayu or magnificent Agni instead. Remember that the noble Sati, who married Shiva earlier, had to kill herself when the world abused her husband as a savage wreathed in serpents.'

'Those were forms he adopted in sport,' she replied. 'I will not allow you to denigrate the lord of my heart, the god who carries the bull banner and the Pinaka bow.' Seeing her begin to turn away in anger, Shiva revealed himself to her in his splendid form and promised to marry her. Thus, Parvati revealed to the world the transcendent power hidden under Shiva's macabre forms. He also showed the world that she was his soulmate in every birth. He had come to her at the very spot where he had burned Kama, brought there by her love and mystic power. This was a divine sport they played in order to show the devas and humanity the eternal bond they shared.

The ascetic Shiva, accompanied by the rishis, went

to her father Himavan, to formally seek her hand in marriage, thereby establishing a convention for mortals to follow. It was not just Parvati who sought to marry him, but he too had come to woo her and seek the blessings of her people to marry her. Their wedding was performed with great pomp and ceremony in the presence of all the gods. And in due course, Shiva's son Kartikeya destroyed Taraka and re-established dharma on earth and heaven.

LESSONS LEARNED

Here, Sati and Parvati show themselves to be equal to Shiva. The great ascetic embraces the life of a householder, seeking to be united with his female half. Though Parvati is rejected by Shiva as a lovely young girl, she wins him over in her ascetic form, making him seek her father's blessings to marry her. Shiva knows that without his Shakti he would become a shava, or corpse. When the two are apart, the world is in chaos and adharma prevails.

In human life too, an ideal couple unites the qualities of logic and forcefulness with those of tenderness and caring. A world that relies solely on the mind and its powers cannot achieve balance without the softening influence of the heart and emotions, nor can it regenerate and flourish. So, the romance of Parvati and Shiva is a story of how feminine strength transforms the world with love. It's also a metaphor for the integration of mind and heart, and of knowledge and love, which is necessary for people to become whole. She brings the divine back into the earthly world by standing firm against her parents' fears and protests. The puranas show Parvati not just as a beautiful maiden but also as a wise soul imbued with the wisdom of the Vedas and philosophy. If Shiva is her guru at times, she is his at others. The seven sages listen to their debates and discover the truths of the universe.

There are many stories of how this marriage of two strong minds results in fiery quarrels, where Parvati stands her ground and retains her own identity. What if Shiva does not wish to have children and the attendant responsibilities? She creates her son, Ganesha, out of her own body and ensures that Shiva accepts him too, even if it requires a fierce battle. Parvati is a role model for modern women in the way she reinvents herself in many forms that are worshipped across the nation. She is Annapurani, the source of nourishment. She is Kamakshi, the goddess with the eyes of love. She is everything creative and powerful. She is the Kundalini Shakti, the inner energy that pushes you to break through barriers and empowers you to reach for a loftier destiny. And whatever her form, her love for her loved ones and for all creation, remains constant.

What does this mean to you? Parvati represents the power that can free you from your bonds, help you to blossom and show you how to love without sacrificing your self-esteem. As more and more women move out of the domestic sphere in order to claim a larger role in the affairs of humankind, she shows you how you can explore your power without compromising on love. In her, you see how you can express force without aggression and love without becoming submissive. We will learn more from the goddesses in the following chapters.

2
The Three Cs

Society has its own way of putting a woman in 'her place'—predominantly the kitchen or the bedroom. You have to fit into people's image of an ideal woman by being soft, sensitive, nurturing, emotional, passive and innocent. The problem begins when 'soft' and 'innocent' imply being gullible and an easy target for bullying, 'sensitive' and 'nurturing' mean sacrificing your own well-being, and 'passive' and 'emotional' imply being a doormat and kowtowing to others' wishes and commands. In other words, you are expected to be at someone's beck and call, a person who clings, cries and cowers, whose purpose in life is to merely cook, clean and care for the children.

This is when you cease to be a woman with needs, ambitions and rights and become a stereotype—fitting into society's expectations for your gender. You are expected to look a certain way and behave a certain way. A desirable woman is one who is small, slim and shapely. God forbid you are heavy or large. 'You need to exercise, woman!' people lecture you. 'You are probably eating too much.' Many industries are flourishing on this premise, as the world seeks to force-fit you into the ideal shape. Diets, boot camps, slimming pills, health warnings—it would seem as if the world will grind to a halt if you weigh slightly more than the numbers on charts drawn up by people who have something to gain from your insecurity.

Society's expectations also extend to your clothes, your activities and everything that makes you who you are. You cannot go out late, you cannot party, you cannot wear skirts, you cannot drink. Society has generously allowed you out of your cage, and you must be careful that you do not exceed your limits and end up being molested or murdered. The victim is the one who is blamed, not the perpetrator as justice would demand. The odds are stacked against you. You face sexist behaviour every day and have to deal with unfair treatment. As a homemaker, you are not paid, nor is your contribution acknowledged or rewarded. On the other hand, the man is lauded because he goes out to work and brings home a salary.

If you do go out to work, due to choice or family circumstances, you are still expected to return home within a few minutes of office closing time. You need to complete your household chores without letting others suffer, for the house remains solely your domain. You may also be encouraged to take up certain 'suitable' jobs—as a teacher perhaps—so that you can come home early. There is also talk of how you will be 'safe' in your job, though at times this is just a light camouflage to keep you from temptation. A job that requires you to work with many young men, as in the information technology industry, may lay you open to temptation, after all! Do these notions sound prehistoric? Well, just search online for stories of working women who are beaten up every day because their husbands think they are being unfaithful. You will be surprised at the number of incidents that turn up, in advanced countries and others alike, both in big cities and small towns. Wealth, education, employment—none of these factors seem to protect a woman from being harassed and in some cases, driven to suicide.

IT'S ALL ABOUT CHOICE

Perhaps you are wondering why you cannot cook or clean if that is what you like doing. There's nothing wrong at all if that is your choice. Speaking up for your rights does not mean that you must go out to work if you do not wish to. That would be taking feminism to an undesirable extreme. Women find fulfilment in playing various roles—as homemaker, as working woman, or as both. Some women choose to be single; others prioritize marriage. Once married, there is another choice to be made—whether to have children or not. Some other women find meaning in a cause or in helping others.

Women, just like men, are allowed to be different, to pursue their own dreams and set their own goals. Not everyone needs to become the president of their company, unless that is what they wish for. The point is that in choosing to be a homemaker, you do not give others carte blanche to treat you with disrespect. Your contribution needs to be valued for what it is—indispensable to the well-being of the family and society. The way you bring up your children determines the future of the world. The home you create provides a peaceful refuge for your family from the stresses of a hostile world. However, even when your home is your primary space, it should not become a cage. You must be free to utilize your talents and pursue your interests, whether it is travelling, theatre or photography.

Not just women, men too can become victims of stereotypes, for they are expected to be tall, bronzed and muscled, leaving the others out in the cold! Is a man less manly because he is a dancer or musician? You probably don't think so, but there are still many notions prevalent in society and media, encouraging men to be rough and ready, rather than caring and nurturing. Helping the wife or taking care of children does not fit into the picture of the macho man, and here too, it is the woman who loses out. The man is afraid to show his feelings as he is brought up to believe that this is a sign of weakness. This leaves the women in his life high and dry, going through the motions of living without getting any validation of their importance in his life. Other markers of so-called manly behaviour are also destructive and disruptive—drinking, drugs, gambling and being promiscuous.

Unfortunately, gender stereotypes have not changed much with time. If you protest against these stereotypes, you are in danger of being called a fishwife, a shrew or a bitch. These words themselves are sexist and derogatory. They make you out to be a whiny, annoying woman, selfish and self-centred, who is always complaining about others and making a big deal of small things. In short, you are everything that is hated and shunned. You probably shudder at the thought of becoming a bitter, angry woman who people avoid. You do not want others to think that you are a big mouth and a troublemaker, or that you are immature and have an attitude problem. Should fear prevent you from speaking up when you have to? Of course not! Trolls attack you merely to keep you quiet and submissive, and prevent you from protesting against injustice. You should challenge these stereotypes and point them out when you see them, hopefully encouraging others to join the revolt.

NOT A DOORMAT OR DRAGON—BE A DIVA!

To achieve the right balance in your life, you must first understand your options. You need not be either a doormat or a dragon, which translates into being submissive or aggressive, respectively. There is another choice—a wiser, smarter, superior choice: To be a diva. This word does not imply that you should throw tantrums or be difficult to please. It indicates that you should be respected as someone who is an achiever in your own way, in what you choose to do. Remember the power within you. No one messes with a goddess!

You are discarding the options of being submissive and aggressive, in order to be assertive. How does this differ from the first two? Let us look at some simple examples.

Perhaps your neighbour is playing music loudly and disturbing you when you are studying for an exam or just trying to relax. How would you react? You may bring out your earmuffs and try to ignore it. Keeping quiet and avoiding the issue is a classic example of passive behaviour which gets you nowhere. Or you may walk up to his door, apologize for ringing his bell, and then stutter as you request him to turn down the volume of his stereo. He is probably not going to listen.

The other extreme is to become aggressive, to tell him that he is always noisy and disruptive: 'I cannot tolerate this! Turn down the volume or else!' you scream.

'Or else what?' he may ask. 'This is my house and I can do what I want within my four walls.' He slams the door in your face. Or worse still, he outshouts you or gets physical. This is not what you would want either, is it?

What does assertive behaviour look like? Remember, this is what you should be aiming for. You look him firmly in the eye, speak in a steady, confident voice, tell him that you are tired, ill or whatever else, and that you find the noise disturbing. 'You may not have realized this and I would appreciate it greatly if you would turn it down.' If he seems to not understand your request, repeat it again. Just stick to the point and stay calm. Do not get annoyed or sidetracked. If he nods and agrees, thank him for obliging you. If he argues, telling you that your carpenter worked at odd hours and kept him awake, acknowledge his complaint and tell him that you will ensure that in future you will limit these activities to reasonable hours. Remember that this is not a single battle for you to win, but a war that will go on. And you may not win the next time! It is always better to open up lines of communication and maintain cordial relationships where possible, as we often live in close proximity to others.

The point is to be clear on where you stand and address issues before you reach your boiling point and begin to rant and rave. If you do find yourself getting angry, postpone the confrontation until you are calmer. This way, you feel more in control of yourself and your situation. You bring down your stress levels and become confident that you can handle future conflicts successfully as well. After all, disagreements are inevitable at work or at home, but you can prevent long-term damages. You need to also consider if you are reacting to the symptoms, and not dealing with the root cause of your anger. You may be shouting at your children for playing music loudly, but the real reason for your annoyance may lie deeper. You may be feeling overwhelmed by all your chores and wish they would offer to help. When they do not, your resentment comes out indirectly and results in a no-holds-barred battle where no one wins.

So, how do you rid yourself of patterns of passive behaviour that leave you resentful and frustrated? Also, how do you prevent your anger from building up and exploding one fine day, resulting in you making bitter enemies over a small matter? The answer lies in learning to be assertive, quickly getting rid of annoyances that drain your energy, and making space for your own health and relaxation. If you are happy and at peace, you are a better person to be around, too. Decide your stance and stick to your rights because they are important to you.

WHAT ARE YOUR RIGHTS?

It may seem strange to be talking about rights when speaking of your family. Isn't life all about compromise and sacrifice, especially when you are a woman? At least, that's what your parents, society and media keep telling you. Well, this is not so advisable if all the compromises and sacrifices come from your end. If you accompany your husband on an obligatory road trip to a remote place without Wi-Fi, he should be willing to accompany you to a destination of your choice. This is not a matter of keeping score, but a way to reciprocate affection. You need not give in always, but should work towards being happy together.

So, to return to the point: What are your rights?

- To speak up for what you think, to do what you wish to do, and to question authority or tradition in a quest to make things better.
- To be free from harassment of any kind.
- To agree or disagree, show happiness or sorrow, to praise or criticize and to free yourself from fears that prevent you from doing these.
- To deal with matters that annoy you before they build up to resentment and aggression.
- To say 'no' to things you do not wish for and let go of the fear of being labelled as 'rude' or 'selfish'.

Pretty basic, right? This is not an over-the-top manifesto to kill all men, as some may wish to present it. Rather, it is an expression of your rightful desire to be respected as a significant, equal human being. It is a sad commentary on society, that you need to reiterate your rights because they have been suppressed for too long, whereas a man can assert these rights without being questioned. Also, remember that each time you kowtow to a bully, you are not only being unjust to yourself but also encouraging the other person to be nasty, greedy and self-centred. It is not going to be easy to speak your mind, though—especially when you are talking to a friend whom you want to please; or when you are addressing someone who has power over you, maybe a parent or a boss. You are immobilized by the fear that he or she will feel threatened and tighten the screws on you. But if you give in, the noose only gets tighter. So what should you do? How do you go about asserting your right to happiness and refuse to be a doormat?

You need to change your habits. Here are the three steps you must take, expressed in the form of three Cs so that they are easy to remember:

CHOOSE. CHANGE. CREATE.

CHOOSE the areas and behaviours you need to modify, the people you must deal with or disconnect from. Learn to say 'no' to requests or situations that harm you or hinder your growth and happiness. Naturally, there will be a reaction—mostly negative. But stay calm and reasonable, and reiterate your 'no', with reasons if necessary. Be open to listening and don't argue endlessly or unnecessarily. If it is a family member or friend, let them know that you care for them but that you need to address your own situation or needs as well. If you need to take a stand at work, weigh the consequences of a 'no'. Reiterate your support to the establishment, check if you can reprioritize your work to take care of the current request, or try and suggest an alternative resource to get the job done.

CHANGE the way you think, feel and act in each specific situation that troubles you. Believe in yourself and your right to happiness. Plan ways in which you can assert yourself. Practise your responses until they become second nature to you. Reading a book or talking to a therapist may show you the path to get started upon, but you need to learn by doing. Use the ideas and examples in this book and try out the methods described, to see what works for you. As you practise being assertive, you learn how to manage your emotions better and gain more control and confidence. These habits will become part of your nature and help you live a more fulfilling life. Stay firm even if you face strong reactions. The path gets easier without doubt and you will be thankful for the change.

CREATE a new 'you' that is happy, peaceful and successful. Reinforce your changed behaviour by remembering that only *you* can take care of yourself. You may have trained yourself and others to behave in a certain way and it is now time to create new patterns to promote your own well-being. Isn't life too fleeting to be wasted in regret and unhappiness?

Allow yourself to dream. Visualize a happier 'you'. Follow your star.

Seems too much? No, you can do it. Change can be stressful but it will help you in the long run. Take the steps at a pace that you find comfortable. Even if you have a relapse, do not worry. You have the rest of your life to get it right, but the sooner you start, the better! If you find the struggle too uphill, you could take the help of a therapist or coach. So wake up, speak up! You have a right to be happy, woman!

> **Tip:** *You cannot complete a marathon on the first day you decide to run. Start slowly, with easy situations and people to say 'no' to. Ask the waiter for a table farther from the noisy one he points you to. Tell the guy who jumps the queue to go to the end of the line. Then move on to handle a dominating husband or colleague.*

Savitri: A Strong Woman

Princess Savitri, who followed her husband Satyavan to Yama's world, is held up as a role model for a chaste wife. She performed fasts for Satyavan, and modern women are expected to do the same, in order to ensure that their husbands enjoy a long life. She is regarded as the ultimate sati, ready to abandon life if Satyavan should die. You may have read her story and wondered if she had no respect for her own life or if she was afraid to live on after his death. Perhaps you have been told that her actions sprang from her great love for Satyavan. But would he have done the same for her if she had died? Is it not more likely that he would have mourned her for a short while and then married a younger woman? Why, then, do I call Savitri a strong woman? Well, read on and you may find that your opinion about her choices changes radically!

Asvapati, the king of Madra, had power and wealth, and enjoyed the love of his people. But the gods had not blessed him and his wife, Malavi, with a child. The king embarked on a long, arduous penance to Savitr, the Sun God, whose golden splendour illuminates the air, the earth and the vault of heaven. It is he who awakens the world in the morning, and at whose command, night arrives. He is the god of sacrifices and is so powerful that no one can resist his will.

The king prayed for many long years, giving up the luxuries of his palace to live the life of an ascetic, seeking a boon from the Golden One. Of course, he sought a son, for kings and mortals in earlier times—like in present day—crave sons, not daughters. They believe that only a son will be able to take care of them. Even when they die, it is the son who will perform the funeral rites to enable them to go to heaven.

Finally, Savitr appeared before the king in a blaze of light, clad in iridescent robes, his hair glowing golden around his face. 'I am pleased with your penance, Asvapati!' he said. 'Ask me for the boon you desire.'

'O God of Light, Lord of Creation!' said the king in adoration. 'Grant me a hundred sons who will perpetuate my line, protect my domain and will light my way to heaven.'

Savitr laughed, for he was wise and he had a lesson to teach humanity. 'Noble king, I bless you with a daughter who will equal a hundred sons,' said the god. And as Asvapati stood bedazzled, the god disappeared as magically as he had come.

Nine months later, Queen Malavi gave birth to a child, a radiant daughter whom they named Savitri after the god who had granted them the boon. As their child grew, her beauty and her intellect shone brightly, inspiring awe and admiration in all who saw her. Alas, this meant that no man had the courage to stand before her and ask for her hand in marriage. Finally, Asvapati granted Savitri permission to find her own groom, for it was an accepted custom for high-born women to seek out the right husband for themselves. 'I know that your wisdom will guide you in finding a worthy husband,' he said.

Savitri set out on a golden chariot, accompanied by soldiers and counsellors, to look for the right suitor. She journeyed far and wide but found none who could win her heart. Was her mission to end in failure then? Finally, she saw the one destined to be her husband— not in the court of a king, but in a forest. For it was in these wild regions that rules gave way to freedom, and a new order could be born, springing from the minds of seers. The forest was where sages lived, surmounting the mundane and providing mankind with new solutions and insights.

Here Savitri came upon King Dyumatsena of Salwa, who had lost his sight and his kingdom, and now lived in exile in the forest. His son, Prince Satyavan, was the embodiment of Truth, as befitted his name, and shone with the lustre of goodness. He too fell in love with the matchless princess. Savitri returned to her father's court, and bowed before him and Narada, the celestial sage who had come to visit their kingdom.

'I have chosen Satyavan, prince of Salwa, who will be a worthy partner in my journey of life,' she said.

When he heard her speak these words, Narada felt a strange sickness seize his soul and he stumbled to a seat where he sat with his eyes closed in prayer.

'What is it, Great Sage?' asked the worried king, when the rishi finally opened his eyes. 'You appear strangely distraught after hearing Satyavan's name. Is he not as virtuous as my daughter describes? Will he not be a faithful husband to her? Guide us, Narada, in making the right decision.'

Narada gathered himself together and replied calmly. 'Savitri is truly a radiant spirit, born through the grace of Savitr,' he said. 'She shows her nobility by choosing not a prince with abundant power and wealth but one who lives in exile—impoverished and isolated. There is no doubt that Satyavan is a worthy groom—as glorious as the full moon, as heroic as Indra, as righteous as Dharma and as forgiving as the earth. But Savitri has committed a grave blunder in choosing him. For, Satyavan will die, this very day, after one year passes! She will enjoy supreme love for one year and then face many, many years of grief. Do you think this brief happiness is worth the sacrifice?'

'Alas, my child, turn away from this terrible fate at once,' said Asvapati to his daughter. 'It is fortunate that your marriage has not taken place as yet and that the devarishi is here in our court to enlighten us. Choose someone else, my daughter, not this ill-fated prince.'

Savitri carefully considered Narada's revelation. And then she spoke, her voice firm and clear. 'All of us who are born must die, father,' she said. 'I have made my choice and I will stand by it. I will fight the odds and win, come what may. Or I will face the consequences with equanimity. Remember that you promised that I could choose my husband. I request you to stand by your word.'

'This noble soul is indeed born on earth to transform men, to uphold dharma even in the face of death,' murmured the rishi, watching as the king begged her fruitlessly to change her decision. He blessed the princess and went his way, leaving the king to come to terms with Savitri's decision.

Seeing that Savitri's will was indomitable, Asvapati sent a golden chariot for Dyumatsena, his wife and son, and welcomed them respectfully to his court. He offered his daughter's hand in marriage to Satyavan. Though startled that the princess should choose someone who lived in the harsh forest, instead of one who could offer her the pleasures of a palace, the Salwa king acceded to the request. The marriage was performed according to religious rites and Savitri cast off her jewellery and rich garments for simple robes, and left with her new family for the forest. Having chosen this life for herself, she devoted herself—body and soul—to life in the wilderness and to the happiness born of true love.

Savitri and Satyavan lived with the rishis in an ashram, where the air was pure and minds were purer still. Here no animals were killed and peace prevailed. The birds and the fish lost all fear of men, and even accepted food from their hands. They led simple lives, meditating on a loftier realm.

Alas, time would stop for no one—not even the virtuous couple. Soon, only four days remained before the dreaded day when Satyavan would die. Savitri's agony was boundless, as only she knew of the prediction and had to bear the pain alone. She decided to take up a vow to challenge his fate, and gave up food and sleep for three days and three nights, preparing herself for the ordeal that was to come. When the sun rose on Satyavan's last day, Savitri accompanied him into the forest where he went every day to cut wood.

'You are too weak with fasting and prayers,' Satyavan protested, seeking to dissuade his wife from going with him into the rough jungle, but she would not be deterred. 'My body is strengthened by my will,' she declared. 'Determination is the basis of every success.'

She followed him with a watchful eye. He completed his task quickly but grew strangely languid in a short while. He lay down to rest, with his head on her lap. Savitri watched, unmoving, her heart flooding with tenderness and growing terror as she sensed that the dark hour was near. Her strong husband, so weakened— she knew that it was a sign of his imminent death.

She sat alone in the forest, her eyes flowing with tears, until Yama's messengers came for Satyavan. But they could not come near him, because Savitri's fierce vow and meditation had created a wall of fire that they could not breach. Yama, the god of death, came there himself, to perform his duty of deciding whether the departing soul would go to swarga or naraka.

Yama, with his dreadful powers, entered the charmed circle around Savitri and she looked up at once, her pure soul allowing her to see the dreaded god. His eyes were red, his robe was red and his intent was clear. 'I am Yama and I have come to claim noble Satyavan's soul,' he said, before bending over the sleeping man and pulling his soul from his body as if it were a mere thread. Satyavan's head fell down heavily on Savitri's lap as life left him. The god turned and walked away, the earth shaking with the force of his steps. Savitri set her husband's head down on a pillow of grass, wiped away her tears and rose to her feet to follow the god.

'You can come no further, child,' Yama said. 'Return to the land of the living and perform your husband's final rites.'

'I am not following you, O Yama,' replied Savitri. 'I am following the love that binds me to Satyavan and will not allow me to be separated from him. When his soul travels with you, mine must too; for it is united with his. And where my soul goes, my body must follow.'

'But what if your husband is a sinner and goes to naraka? What then? Will you follow him there, too?' he asked, for he was also the god of justice and truth, and he loved nothing more than to discuss the Eternal Law.

Savitri was unfazed, and replied, 'I will follow him to heaven or hell, in life or death; for, that is the promise I made when I married him.'

'Your resolve impresses me,' said Yama. 'Ask for a boon—any boon except the life of your husband.'

'Great God, please restore the eyesight that Satyavan's father lost so that he may be mighty as before, and regain his kingdom,' she said, and the god was pleased to grant the boon, before going his way.

However, she still followed Yama, though he told her that their path was long and torturous and that she would not be able to keep up with him. 'The wise say that when we walk seven steps with another, we become friends. I have walked many steps with you now and claim your friendship, Great God,' she said. He smiled at her and nodded in acceptance. 'Righteous men show mercy even to their enemies when they seek their protection,' she continued. 'You are much greater than a mortal and are the god of dharma. In the name of our friendship, I entreat you to show me mercy.'

'I am pleased with your words and grant you another boon. But remember that the dead cannot come to life again.'

'Then grant my father Asvapati the boon of a hundred sons that he asked for when praying to Savitr,' she said, seeking always the welfare of others. Yama granted her this boon as well and asked her again to turn back.

'Great son of the Sun God!' she said. 'You are the upholder of truth in the universe and are hence known as Dharmaraja. You determine when lives must end— a necessary task for the world to survive—discharging your duty without fear or favour. I am blessed to be able to travel in your company, O Yama.'

'People always rage at me for taking away their loved ones,' said Yama. 'I am astonished and delighted that a human should praise me as you do.'

Savitri matched her step with his, and stayed calm and composed. 'You are merciful, generous and kind,' she said. 'And as there is no fear among friends, I wish to seek your answer to my question. It is known that the three stages in life are those of a student, a householder and finally, one who renounces the pleasures of life. Satyavan has just entered the second and most important stage of a householder. Why have you flouted your own law by coming for him so soon?'

'His life has ended, as was determined when he was born,' Yama replied. 'But your wisdom and your piety have impressed me so much that I grant you another boon.'

'Let not the royal line of my father-in-law be broken,' she said. 'Let his kingdom be extended by Satyavan's sons.'

The Lord of Death smiled, for he had purposely not specified that she could not ask for her husband's life. He knew that by granting her this boon, he was also granting her Satyavan's life, for he would not be able to bear any children if he were no longer alive.

'So be it!' he said, and Savitri's face lit up with joy. 'I return your husband to you and bless you both with eternal happiness. You have proved that there is nothing a woman cannot achieve with her wisdom, her resolve and her love. Your dharma protects the world. You are the embodiment of truth, and hence, Satyavan's true partner. You have won over death, Savitri, with a love that surpasses the power of tapasya. No woman who hears your story can doubt that you are brave, free and indomitable—a righteous model for all who live on earth.'

The joyous princess joined her hands in worship to Yama and returned to where her husband lay on the cold ground. She stroked his face with fond hands and wept in thanksgiving as the breath of life warmed his body once more. When Satyavan awoke, she took him by his hand and led him back to the ashram. His father had recovered his sight and his people had arrived to take him back to be king, as they had driven out the usurper. Savitri told them about her encounter with Yama and the boons he had granted. There was much rejoicing as these boons came true. Savitri had many children to complete their happiness, and Satyavan succeeded his father to the throne. Sages and courtiers, families and kings alike, sang praises of Savitri, who had encountered death and brought back her husband from its dire shores.

A ROLE MODEL

What do you think of Savitri now? Do you still regard her as a weak woman who believed that she was worth nothing without her husband? Or do you perceive her in a new light, as a strong woman who stands by her choice and wins over adversity? Though Narada proclaims that Satyavan must die, she recognizes the prince as her true love and decides to abide by her decision, come what may. Then she fights against fate, with an indomitable will that endows her with divinity. How does she prepare herself for her task? She undertakes a vrata, which is not a meaningless ritual, but the honing of her spirit, through which she empowers herself to face the impending crisis. Vyasa, when he narrates her story in the *Mahabharata*, emphasizes this by not portraying her as someone who needs to be rescued, but as a strong woman who can transmute death through her love and persistence. She is courageous, intelligent, enterprising, free-thinking—every quality that a woman today needs to exhibit in order to claim her place in life. Savitri is not decorative but decisive. She uses not pathos, but courage and logic to establish a rapport with a superior power to achieve what she wants. Perhaps you can think of her when you are striving for success in your organization!

Throughout the story, it is Savitri's will and her choice that dominate. This is not a tale extolling a woman's chastity as it is often portrayed. Savitri represents action—the power of Shakti who remains awake when Shiva is in deep meditation, or in Satyavan's case, the sleep of death. She takes on the role of protector, whose love is so pure that even death is powerless before it. She is the destroyer too, as she demolishes Yama's resolve to take away her husband. Savitri is both Purusha (the male energy) and Prakriti (the female energy), working to convert untruth into truth, and mortality into immortality. She shows us that a woman is not just about caring and sensitivity, for that would limit her to the domestic sphere. She enhances her willpower through self-discipline, so that she can triumph over all obstacles she encounters. The princess and future queen is a role model, not just of fidelity and love, but of dignity and drive. She is not a mindless slave but an ardhangini—the other half—or even more than half of her man; she is someone who claims half of the responsibilities and rights in society. Savitri shows us how we can command respect from all who meet us—as she does from her family, the sages and the rulers.

Often, our ancient beliefs, embodied in epics like the *Mahabharata,* are corrupted by smaller minds. As a result, a woman is regarded as weak and an inferior adjunct to the husband, regardless of his worth or his moral fibre. Savitri scorches opposition with the power of her inner fire and does not allow her life to end on the pyre of her husband.

Here, let us consider the position of a woman whose husband dies. She may not be forced to commit sati as in earlier regressive times. But instead of death, she is often forced into a life of continued oppression. Society does not want her to marry again, to wear fine clothes and jewellery, or participate in happy occasions. She loses her value as she is defined only by her relationship to a man. Warped minds may even blame her for his death, saying that she failed in her duty to protect him by performing the mandated rituals.

What is this, if not sexism? A man who loses his wife is never denigrated in this way. Let us admire the puranic Savitri for her strength and not use her story to criticize women today. As it is, we live in what the puranas call 'the darkest age' when gods no longer walk the earth.

Religion, as you can see, can either be misused as a means to suppress people on the basis of gender or class, or it can be used to provide a framework for making fair and ethical choices.

Savitri, then, is a good role model, for she establishes her right to choose—which is the very essence of feminism. She chooses a course of action and then acts on it, as we must too. Let us reclaim Savitri's space for ourselves and follow her path to self-empowerment.

3
A Homemaker Is Not a Slave

Megha does not work. She gave up her bank job when her daughter was born because her mother had passed away and her mother-in-law was not willing to help. Megha was not willing to entrust her infant to a crèche and her bank also could not offer her part-time or flexible hours of work. Even if the rules permitted it, her boss would not believe that she was working unless she did so before his eyes. She quit her job, telling herself that she could return to work when her child entered school. But then, she had another child, a son, and her husband told her to wait until both of them grew up. However, she was drawn deeper into the responsibilities of being a full-time mother and wife. She told herself that her children would grow into well-balanced, happy adults when brought up by a stay-at-home mom, as people often told her. Megha's working friends told her she was lucky, for they were answerable both at home and at work. In time, though, she found that the reality was sobering. Her children have grown into surly teenagers, who are rude, patronizing and self-obsessed. To them, she is a 'maid' whose opinions do not matter. She has no money, no job and nothing to bring to the table. 'I will never be like her. I will have a career and pots of money,' says her daughter. Where did Megha go wrong?

Her husband merely laughs when she complains, and says, 'Be honest. You are not a great role model for the next generation, are you?' Megha is hurt and cries her eyes out when she is alone. So, is this what happens when you decide to give your children and home all your love and energy? She has lost everything—their respect and her own self-esteem. Not to speak of the humiliation of having to beg for money if she needs to go out occasionally with her friends or get her hair coloured. She spoke to her aunt about feeling demeaned and unhappy, but her aunt is not supportive or even understanding. 'Just look at your cousin Neela,' she says. 'Her husband gets drunk often and beats her up. She suspects that he is having an affair with a colleague and is afraid he will leave her and her children destitute. Your husband does none of these things. So what are you complaining about? Don't foolishly consider divorce or something. You will be an outcast in our family and in society. And what will you live on?' Megha feels worse now, cornered and rebellious. Is she worth nothing on her own? Should she just bend her head and plod on—a slave for life?

Perhaps you can sympathize with Megha. You are in your thirties, forties or fifties, with nowhere to go. Your husband never helps you with the kids or the chores. You do not have a moment to yourself, while he has his clubs and his dinners. You feel like an unpaid maid and are always tired and resentful. You deal with his mother, his children, chores like cooking, cleaning and paying bills, and then when you are ready to zonk out in bed, he gets romantic. Your home is not a sanctuary of love and support, but a hostile and demeaning environment. You are taken for granted, and unappreciated. You are held responsible for your children's behaviour and are under constant pressure to look young and showcase a perfect home. What if your husband takes up with a younger woman? You have nothing you can call your own—no job or money set aside for your old age. You struggle with your weight and your insecurity, wondering if your family will discard you when you are no longer needed.

Perhaps you are like Megha's cousin Neela—subjected to physical or emotional abuse. After all, crimes against women have more than doubled in the last decade in India, with a new complaint coming in every two minutes. In 2016, 'cruelty by husbands and relatives' topped this list as per the National Crime Records Bureau data. Social workers and lawyers say that for every woman who complains, there is at least one who suffers in silence, due to social stigma or insecurity regarding the future. Also, do not assume that this is confined to the poorer sections. Many women whose marriages seem picture-perfect are in fact leading sordid lives behind closed doors. Parents of these abused women often turn a blind eye to their plight, telling them, 'You must be patient and do everything it takes to make your marriage work.' What more can you expect in a society rooted in patriarchy, where women are regarded as inferior to men? Lawmakers, the police and even judges often think that a man is justified in beating his wife if she disrespects him or his parents, neglects her home or children, or does not cook to their satisfaction. As a mother, you are expected to raise perfect kids in a vicious world where their role models are often the rich, powerful and arrogant. Your husband blames the demands of his job for neglecting his parental role. 'What are you whining about when you spend your day lolling around at home?' he snaps when you try to tell him how you feel. 'You are not the one struggling to make a living, worrying about your job every day. Try working all hours like me and sacrificing even weekends for travel, meetings and workshops.' He is under stress and his punching bag is his wife, who is trained to be passive. At times, he may feel guilty and promise to help out, but things rarely change. In fact, his guilt may prompt him to push back at you violently in an attempt to shut you up.

A woman who faces abuse daily, soon accepts it as the norm. That is the reason you keep reading of educated women even in advanced societies putting up with years of abuse at their partner's hands. Maybe what holds you back from divorce is the fear of the stigma attached, or of living alone. You are afraid that you will be blamed and ostracized. You have no place to go, no job. And you often feel guilty, wondering if something you did is the reason for your current situation. Maybe you are simply not a good mother or wife as your husband often tells you. Your fear and self-doubt may be carried over from childhood when parents or teachers made you feel that you were not good enough. You are so afraid of being rejected that you bend over backwards to please people.

Ultimately, you realize that your life lacks meaning and purpose and that your role is limited to being a maid or a doormat. How can you go on like this? Is there nothing you can do to pull yourself out of this morass of self-pity and despair? Of course, there is. Let's find out how.

APPLY THE THREE Cs TO YOUR LIFE

1. The first C: Choose

- Identify the areas in which you would like to improve your life. Do you always use words or phrases of apology and uncertainty, such as 'sorry', 'I'm afraid', 'maybe', or 'not sure'? Do you put yourself down by telling someone that you are not good at something, or that he or she knows more than you do? Do you seek permission constantly for something you want to do or take the blame for a mistake that is not yours?
- You need to gain the confidence to assert yourself and claim your space. Start the process by reiterating your rights as a human being.
- You have the right to quality relationships, where you can say 'no' to toxic behaviours and stay in control. You are empowered to confront people and problems, instead of letting them overwhelm you and cause you pain.
- You have the right to prioritize your physical and emotional needs, your well-being and health, and to bounce cheerfully out of bed in the morning.

In Megha's case, she decided to put her child's well-being first and give up her job. Other women may do so because they have grown tired of the rat race or because they wish to invest more time in building relationships at home. These decisions are highly personal and no one has the right to question or criticize you. However, keep in mind that there may be ways to keep working and take a break only when you need to.

Let us first focus on your home life. The following are some tell-tale signs, which indicate that you may be in an unequal relationship:

- Are you afraid to be honest with your partner as you think he will not like what you say? Do you feel your opinion matters less than his?
- Have you given up your personal desires and ambitions, your hobbies and friends, in order to fit into his concept of the ideal partner? Are you totally dependent on him for your physical and emotional well-being?
- Have you reached a stage where you feel that there is no use speaking up as your partner will anyway do only what he wants to?
- Are you quick to agree to his decisions even when they may go against what you believe? Are you afraid that he will leave you if you voice your opinion?

Did you say 'yes' to one or more of these questions? That may well indicate that you are in an abusive relationship, where abuse may not necessarily be physical. It may constitute hurtful remarks or disrespect. You may be making excuses for your partner's behaviour by telling yourself that he didn't mean it or that he was under stress. If this is true and he truly loves you and is committed to you, then he will support a change that will ensure your happiness. He will recognize that the two of you are equals in your marriage and that insulting you is not acceptable.

It is better to set boundaries in place during the early years of your marriage in order to ensure an equable relationship. Start the journey the way you wish to continue. Encourage your partner to share in the housework and do not criticize him if his contribution is less than perfect. The division of labour will never be fifty-fifty, but you should keep working towards something that makes both of you happy. In the first flush of love, you may want to display your feelings by doing everything for him, but this will be hard to sustain, especially when children enter the picture. A child completely changes the way you live and think. Your priorities shift and your life gets more exhilarating and exasperating at the same time. And to satisfactorily perform your role as a mother, you need a partner who helps you out so that you do not break under the pressure.

2. The second C is Change

Let us talk of children and your relationship with them as we move on to the next step—Change. Do your children respect what you do? Do they value your love and tireless nurturing? Are they good human beings who can take care of themselves and of others too, if the need arises? If they are like Megha's children, then obviously you need to take corrective steps at once.

Consider, for instance, that your adolescent son constantly leaves his dirty clothes on his bedroom floor and not in the basket earmarked for the purpose. You have told him about this several times but have allowed him to get away with his behaviour. But now you have reached the end of your patience and have to stop yourself from shouting at him. You feel stressed and martyred. You are afraid that you will end up screaming at him and criticizing his laziness, his academic performance, his friends and whatnot.

Many women resort to passive-aggressive behaviour, saying 'yes' to being exploited and then complaining behind the person's back. This happens when you are uncomfortable about expressing your needs and feelings directly. Instead, you show your anger through actions or sarcasm. The problem with this style of expression is that you will inevitably damage your relationship, leading perhaps to a breakdown in communication.

Would it not be better to speak up now, so that both of you can retain your self-respect? You are not trying to hurt your son; just preserving your emotional health. You are not being selfish or bullying him; just asking him to respect your feelings. Standing up for your rights does not, in any way, harm his own.

So, try to be assertive with him. Look him in the eye, tell him firmly that clothes not dropped in the hamper will not get washed. Period. If he laughs or quibbles, repeat what you said. And then stick to it. Do not start picking up after him, collecting clothes from the floor or his gym bag. He will soon get the message that if he needs clean clothes, he needs to put them in the hamper. Cruel? No, practical! You will be at peace, not fuming. You will feel good, reasserting your claim to respect as an individual who knows what she wants and why. So, do not give up at any cost. The first time may be difficult, but think of all the heartburn you will save yourself in future. Keep reinforcing this behaviour suitably so that neither of you falls back into your old ways.

Being a wife and mother is tough, as you know from personal experience. Doing all the housework yourself is exhausting and tedious. And no one thanks you or pays you for the job. It would be nice if they occasionally acknowledged that their clothes do not get washed and ironed by themselves or that the halwa they like so much does not make itself. Just as they love being praised for their achievements in school or at work, they must understand that the patient woman who keeps things moving smoothly at home needs a hug too.

It's always better to address issues at the earliest, instead of waiting for your resentment to boil over. Change your behaviour before reaching a stage where you begin to rant: 'Does anyone know or care how much I do for the family?' They do *know*, of course, whether they acknowledge it or not. But how does that help you? Take the practical approach instead. Tell them that you expect them to give you the same respect and love that you give them; that they should care for your well-being just as you care for theirs; and that if they do not oblige, you will not hesitate to speak up about it.

Catch Them Young

Encourage your children to help you with the chores, making certain tasks their responsibility. Younger ones can fold clothes and dust shelves. Older ones can do the laundry—how much effort does it take to sort clothes and load the washing machine? They can pick up groceries and clean the car/bike. After all, they are going to ask to borrow your vehicle pretty soon!

'But should children do chores?' you ask, regarding it as some form of child labour. What will your mother-in-law or your neighbours say?

Look at it this way. This training does not merely help you; it enables them to be self-sufficient and take care of others too, if needed. You can reward them with an allowance and if they do not perform their chores, take away their phones until the job is done. They may complain that the job is boring, disgusting or repetitive. Simply remind them that you have been doing it for years and thank them for helping out. Never give them what they want if they ask for it rudely. Stop picking up after them. Put their things in a corner of their room and make weekly inspections to see that the room is clean. Do not facilitate their laziness or forgetfulness by doing what they 'forget' to do. Actions have consequences in the real world and the sooner they realize that, the better their life will be. You can help your children because of your love for them, but do not make it a habit that will encourage them to take you for granted.

Initially, especially if your children are grown up and not used to helping, there will be protests. Be patient but persistent. If your son refuses to pick up his things—do not brood and then do it yourself (passive behaviour). Do not throw a tantrum and shout at him (aggressive behaviour), only to apologize later. Do not bang cupboards noisily and do the cleaning up, hoping he will get the message (passive-aggressive behaviour). Just remind him calmly that he has to do his chores and that you are accepting no excuses. This is assertive behaviour that you must practise and perfect.

Husbands Need to Help too

Perhaps you are wondering why your husband needs to help when he already has a heavy workload outside the home and may be very tired. But how will he bond with his children if he does not do stuff for them or with them? Why can't he help you in the weekends, instead of spending endless hours watching TV or hanging out with friends? So, ask him for help. He can do the dusting, remove cobwebs from ceilings, or learn some cooking, so that he can help out in a pinch. Offer him some suggestions and let him choose. You may find that he really doesn't mind the chores and this will be a big help to you over time. Or tell him when you feel overwhelmed and ask him to watch the kids so you can have a peaceful cup of tea or simply listen to music. Do not lash out by saying, 'You never do anything to help!' or 'You are always goofing off with friends while I'm on duty 24x7.' Such statements only result in endless debates on when he helped you last, or how much time he spends with friends. Tell him that you would appreciate it if he bought the vegetables from the Sunday market. He may reply that he did so once or twice and you criticized him, saying that the brinjal was dried up or that he had bought too many oranges. Instead of getting into an argument over this, offer to make a list with exact quantities next time and guide him on how to pick fresh vegetables and fruits. Both of you win this way.

When your husband shares in the housework, you feel less stressed. Conflicts are reduced and you feel more relaxed—and romantic! Give him a chance to show that he is sensitive to your needs. Appreciate the smallest effort he makes in that direction. He will show you what he is capable of!

What if the two of you have too many issues to be resolved? You could probably start off by setting aside half an hour for discussions, using a timer if necessary. Then move on to other things and refrain from getting into a tit-for-tat situation. Remember that it is worthwhile to try saving a relationship than to tear it apart. You have to start changing old patterns before it reaches a point when one of you decides to dissolve the marriage. Imagine the trauma involved in giving up a settled life, looking for ways to cut expenses, taking on a full-time job (if you had quit one, or never had one) and probably facing life alone. Act promptly to solve issues instead. Look for information and support on women's forums and websites. Increasingly, social media is being used as a platform to seek help. And you can google anything, from re-entering the workforce to age-appropriate chores for children.

3. Create: The third C

You have realized by now that you owe it to yourself to be strong and empowered. When you begin to feel like a victim, it's a sign that you must change your behaviour and that of others. Take time out for yourself, clearing your to-do list of everything except items that are urgent. Get help, or hire someone to lighten your load, renegotiate commitments if possible and affirm to yourself that you will not become a doormat. When you begin to change your life's patterns, you will find it easier to spot problem-areas and handle them more effectively.

Your issues with peripheral figures in your life—in-laws, parents, relatives and neighbours—need to be addressed too. It may take some time for people to recognize that you are setting boundaries and sticking to them. At first, they are not likely to be happy about the change, but will gradually begin to accept the new 'you'. If they do not, you may have to decide whether you should rid yourself of such black holes that swallow up your confidence and your spirit. Avoid those who do not accept your right to a happy life. Remember that your seeking others' approval for your actions indicates that you think your opinion is less important than theirs. How can this be? You are intelligent. You are the best judge of what is right for you. Even if you make a mistake, it is okay, for you will learn from it.

Just the fact that you are browsing through this book shows that you are tired of feeling weak, timid or exploited. Continue reading and you will realize that many of your fears can be tackled. Practise saying 'no' in different situations— to tiresome appeals for money or time, and to disrespect. Repeat it as many times as needed. Avoid the stress that results from immediately saying 'yes' without thinking. When possible, plan your answer ahead of time so you do not feel guilty or doubtful later.

Start with easy steps. Say 'no' to a friend who forces you to have a slice of cake when you have already told her you do not want it. Use powerful words, saying that you 'do not' cheat on your diet, rather than you 'cannot'. This leaves no room for debate and makes it clear that you will not break your rule. If she persists, remove yourself from the situation, for she obviously believes that she can wear you down by persisting.

ENJOY THE REWARDS

When you say 'no' to an oft-repeated request, you feel free and empowered. You are no longer a martyr who drags herself through a situation because she did not have the resolve to refuse in the first place. Set boundaries that you are ready and able to defend, and start with just one or two people at first. Continue to develop your assertive skills. Establish a support network. Seek outside help if the situation becomes dangerous.

As your confidence increases, you find that you enjoy better physical and mental health and are better able to manage emotions. Stay committed to the new 'you' and hone your responses through trial and error. Visualize the joy and freedom that you will enjoy, when you give to others because you *want* to and not because you *have* to. It's vital that you achieve a state of happiness before trying to make others happy.

If you have a daughter, become a role model for her as she may already be under immense social pressure to dress and behave as others want her to. Do not allow her to lose her voice and be forced to play a submissive role. Encourage her to express her opinions, to stand up to bullying and acquire skills that will make her a confident, empowered individual. Do not pass on to her your own issues of self-image and your concerns about weight or wrinkles that would make her believe that appearance is the be-all and end-all of a woman's life. If you have a son, make him understand that every person—man or woman—has to be valued and respected. Period.

You know how you (and Megha) can begin to make your lives more fulfilling, don't you?

Do not let people convince you that you are a bad mother for laying down rules for your children. You are in fact making them better people and giving them the foundation for a happier life. Step back slightly and you will realize that this is the advice you will give your friend if she is in your position. As a caring individual you often find it easier to speak up for someone you love rather than for yourself.

Tip: *Don't feel guilty about your changed behaviour. Don't be defensive or relapse into your earlier patterns of submissiveness.*

Let us return to the celestial couple, Shiva and Parvati, and discover how they deal with their disagreements.

Shiva versus Parvati: The Dice Game

Shiva married Parvati and they were blissfully happy together. Or, were they? After all, they were so different from each other. She had lived all her life in a palace whereas he was perfectly happy living on the cremation grounds. She anointed her body with sandal paste; he with ashes. She wore silks and rubies; he donned animal skins and emerald serpents. She was young and passionate, while he was as ancient as the hills, with the soul of a hermit. In addition to these differences, there were many contradictions within Shiva himself. At times, he wished Parvati to be his yogini; at others, he wanted her to be his kamini. He was an amalgam of disparate entities—Parvati's slave and Kama's enemy, husband and ascetic, the god of life and death, the giver of ecstasy and enlightenment. When he was so conflicted, could there be any lack of differences? He tried to teach Parvati the scriptures but she covered his eyes in play and plunged the world in chaos. Could it have been easy to resolve the quarrels between a lively, young wife and the god of destruction?

Narada maharishi, who appeared at key junctures

of time in order to shape destiny, suggested that Shiva and Parvati play a game of dice to spend their time pleasantly. 'Let us have wagers to make the game more interesting. I will stake my earrings against your pearls,' said Shiva. He won the first game and happily took away her lustrous necklace. She staked her gold waist belt next and he won this too, with the next roll of the dice. But then the tide turned. Now, it was she who won and asked that he hand over his earrings. But he refused to concede defeat, saying that as the God of gods he could never lose. 'Let us continue playing, beautiful one!' he said to her.

His devotees clamoured in his support, saying that she should seek his forgiveness for implying that she could defeat him. 'Worship him humbly, Goddess, just as all of us do. Have you forgotten that you won him as your husband only after severe penances?' She ignored them, knowing that they were envious that she had weaned Shiva away from his spiritual discussions with them by means of her youth and beauty.

Parvati was angry that Shiva was flouting the rules they had agreed on, but decided to remain silent for the moment. Next, he staked his drum and lost it. He wagered his snake, his trident and his bull, Nandi, and lost them all, one by one. 'Pay up!' she demanded. But he refused, declaring that no one could ever defeat him. 'No one can defeat you, it's true—except me!' she countered. Shiva saw that she grew lovelier when she grew angrier, and continued to provoke her. However, when she persisted in her demand, he lost his temper and destroyed the light of the sun, plunging the world into darkness. The moon and stars appeared in the sky, but Shiva blotted their light out as well.

Parvati now lost her patience and proclaimed that she now owned everything that was his. He would soon lose his loincloth as well. 'Sacrilege!' shouted the sages. 'You seem to be deluded by love, Devi,' they said. 'Do not forget that Shiva burned the love god, Kama, to ashes. Also remember that you are a mere woman—insignificant before his cosmic power!' The Goddess silenced them with a glare and gestured at the skies to bring back the sun. 'Though you are the Lord of all creation,' she said to Shiva, 'you have to honour the rules we play by. You have lost many times and must now pay your dues.' Realizing that she would not bend to him, Shiva opened his third eye in anger. 'Do you think I'm afraid?' she retorted. 'Am I Kama, or the demon Andhaka, or the triple city of Tripura, that you burned when you became angry?'

Unhappy with the turn of events, Shiva retreated to the forest to meditate. Vishnu came to him and offered to help him defeat Parvati. The God of Kailasa returned to play the game and astonished Parvati by winning each throw of the dice. 'Are you cheating, Lord?' she asked him finally, but he refused to answer. She stood up, ready to forsake the game, when Vishnu appeared with a smile and confessed that he had indeed manipulated the dice to make Shiva win. 'So, neither you nor he has won or lost, Devi, as the game itself is an illusion. Give up your anger,' he said, before taking his leave.

'All material things are only illusions,' said Shiva. 'And I am above everything that you preside over as Prakriti, including food and other fruits of nature.' Enraged that her powers should be dismissed as a mirage, Parvati lost her temper and said, 'If I am just maya, let us see how you and the world survive without me! You insult me and my powers, mocking me instead of showing love and respect. What can I expect of a god who lives on the cremation grounds, wearing animal skins? You scoff at love and life that I hold dear, and wear skulls and ashes that symbolize death. I can no longer live with you, O Shiva!'

She then stormed away, leaving the world to suffer a terrible drought that led to universal hunger. Time stood still, the seasons no longer changed and life floundered on a barren earth. Humans, gods and demons alike suffered, as there was no food anywhere. They wept and prayed to the Goddess to save them. The sages who had scorned Parvati now realized that their souls could not survive without their bodies. No prayers could be said when their stomachs cramped in hunger. 'Come back and help us, Annapurani, Goddess of nourishment,' they cried.

Seeing the extent of their suffering, Parvati returned to earth, appearing in the divine town of Kashi to bless them. Shiva also presented himself before her with his bowl and the Goddess filled it to the brim. His action showed the world that life was meaningless without the power of Shakti, who sustains the world and imbues life with joy. The divine pair retired once more to Kailasa, where they ruled side by side, acknowledging that each of them needed the other. The game was over and they had successfully enlightened the world.

LESSONS LEARNED

Conflicts, conquests, conciliation…Why did our ancient bards spin these tales, showing gods and goddesses engaged in quarrels and reconciliation just like humans? Perhaps it was to show us different emotions and motivations at play, and the final victory that we may achieve when we stand up for our beliefs. Men and women are equal, and each individual is entitled to his or her own ideas and desires. And it is when opposites come together that we are able to create something extraordinary. Though Shiva and Parvati together are known as Ardhanarishwara, it was only when they separated into Purusha and Prakriti that Creation happened.

Life, in a way, is like a game that is to be played by the rules. We have no control over which way the dice will flip. All we can do is give the game our best and continue playing with zest, whether we win or lose. Our ability to adapt to circumstances and adversities determines our success and happiness.

As the great dramatist Shakespeare said,

All the world's a stage,
And all the men and women merely players.

Make sure that you play the game the right way, giving no quarter to foes and detractors.

4

A Working Woman,
Not a Pushover

Mary is turning thirty this year and is not married. Her parents have given up trying to arrange an alliance and she has not been able to find the right person herself. She has been focusing on her work in a healthcare company for the last ten years. But unfortunately, she has not risen high enough in the organization. Her father tells her that she has nothing much to show for 'sacrificing' her personal life for her career. She has interviewed for jobs in other companies but found that she will not be gaining much by making the jump. Is there something wrong in her approach that prevents her from achieving success?

Sheela goes to work now that her kids are grown up. She has been waiting for quite a while to use her skills at the workplace and gain some financial freedom. However, she has come to realize that she has merely added one more job to her existing ones as 'cook', 'cleaner', 'wife' and 'parent'. She is run off her feet trying to perform her roles at work and home to everyone's satisfaction and has grown increasingly frustrated and fatigued. Her children and husband do not help with the chores or the household management. Her job sometimes requires her to stay late and she feels torn between guilt and anger when she rushes home and meets her family's accusing eyes as she starts making dinner. They cannot afford a cook and she is also diffident about giving an outsider the house key. Sheela is exhausted all the time and wonders if she is not as capable as she had thought she was. Her job is interesting and she can visualize being successful there. But she also feels guilty that she is neglecting her home and family. Should she quit her job and her new-found independence? The stress is killing her and her husband is unhappy that she orders dinner when she is late.

Just as Mary found that her commitment to her job does not help her advance, many working women have found that their rewards are not commensurate with their experience or capabilities. While girls do extremely well in school and college, this success is usually not carried forward in the workplace. They find it tougher at every stage, from entry point to senior levels. All that ambition and academic success—where does it all go? Here are some hard facts exposing the ugly reality where women and the workplace are concerned:

1. *It's more difficult to get a job:* If you are young and fresh out of college, the human resource manager suspects that you will not be as committed to a career as your

male counterpart. You may quit to get married or take a maternity break. He prefers to hire a man, even though he may be less qualified and capable, because he is certain that he will be more likely to stay in the job.

2. *You earn less:* A recent study by the Ministry of Statistics and Programme Implementation, India, shows that a woman earns perhaps 30 per cent less than an equally educated male candidate over a lifetime of work.[1] You are often regarded as a doubtful commodity and forced to prove that you can deliver results, starting all over again when you change jobs. Men may look to you when they want someone to take notes or do the 'simpler' tasks. Clients may ignore you and address a male junior, assuming that he is your superior, just because he is a male.

3. *You are not given credit:* Often, even when you drive a team's success, the credit is given to the men in your team, as per the general perception about what men and women are capable of achieving. Sometimes your success is attributed to a perceived closeness with the boss. You may also be prone to downplaying your role as you are taught to be self-effacing. If you fail, however, the price you pay is higher, as it merely reinforces popular belief.

4. *You are afraid to negotiate:* Most women find it hard to claim their dues in pay or position as they fear that they will appear pushy and lose the job. If you are efficient and

---

[1]Gender wage pay gap: Women graduate in India earns 24% less than her male counterpart. (2018, June 05). Retrieved from https://www.businessinsider.in/gender-wage-pay-gap-women-graduate-in-india-earns-24-less-than-her-male-counterpart/articleshow/64460159.cms

ambitious, you are regarded as aggressive and manipulative. Employers are reluctant to accept females in strong positions, as they perceive them to be hard as nails and lacking in social skills. The same stance in a man, however, is easily accepted—a result of skewed social attitudes.

5. ***You underplay your ambition:*** You may not wish to be labelled a feminist, a word that is often mistakenly used to mean a strident woman who is a 'taker' instead of a 'giver'. If you make a point forcefully, men often smirk and speculate whether it is 'the wrong time of the month'.

6. ***Landmines at every step:*** You must be nice as befits a woman, but not too nice, which makes you seem lackadaisical or gullible. You must be a nurturer, but not a hands-on mother, as you will then lose focus on your job. You must be confident and capable, but not shrill and shrewish.

7. ***Trying to do it all:*** You think you must be the perfect mother, wife, housekeeper, employee and boss. However, this is not possible when you have only a finite amount of time and energy. You are forced to make choices between work and home, and between your own needs and those of others, ending up dealing with your own guilt as well as flak from others. (Read more about this in the next chapter.)

8. ***The likeability factor:*** When a man is successful, everyone likes him. However, this is not the case with a woman. Likeability is a key factor when it comes to advancement in both personal and professional spheres. So, if your ambition makes your seniors think that you can't work well with others, you may lose that plum position you have been aiming for.

9. ***Focusing on marriage over career:*** Society brainwashes you into believing that your first priority is to catch the right man before the world runs out of them! Keeping this in mind, you start turning down opportunities, responsibilities, leadership positions, transfers—much before you need to.

So, does all this mean that you should not have a career? If you do take the leap and begin working, should you compromise on pay and position, so as to not rock the boat too much? Of course not! An article in the Harvard Business Review asks if a woman's high-status career hurts her marriage, and provides the answer: 'Not if her husband does the laundry!'[2] Sheryl Sandberg, the Chief Operating Officer of Facebook, says in her TED Talk: 'One, sit at the table. Two, make your partner a real partner. And three, don't leave before you leave.'[3] She advises women to participate in decision-making, to make their partners contribute to household tasks, and to not make decisions, such as taking a break to have a child, before they are needed.

So, you should keep pushing back at these obstacles—both internal and external—and join forces with other women to help improve conditions for women. You just have to be smarter and play your cards right.

---

[2]Barling, A. B. (2017, October 31). Does a Woman's High-Status Career Hurt Her Marriage? Not If Her Husband Does the Laundry. Retrieved from https://hbr.org/2017/05/does-a-womans-high-status-career-hurt-her-marriage-not-if-her-husband-does-the-laundry

[3]Sandberg, S. (2010). Why We Have too Few Women Leaders. Retrieved from http://www.mmryan.net/archive/idea/ted/sandbergsheryl/transcript.pdf

Let us apply the three Cs to see how we can tackle the many issues you face.

1. CHOOSE to get ahead

Speaking up for what you need or think, is the first rule for advancement. Studies have shown that women are often hesitant to voice their opinions during meetings.[4] Even when they say something, they do not articulate it forcefully or back up their opinion with evidence. They allow themselves to be interrupted or go off at a tangent, leaving their audience confused and unconvinced. If they are challenged by others or even if they lose their attention, they freeze.

'I do not like to fight and would rather avoid it,' you may respond. 'I feel scared, anxious, alone, outnumbered. How can I go on then?' Standing up for something is not fighting. Even if you are rebuked, there is no need to panic as a contrary opinion may still stimulate debate and result in better solutions. Do not brood or doubt yourself, for you are the only one who can speak for what you think. You should voice your idea if you have one, though you may be shy or afraid that someone will pounce on you. Try speaking up at the next meeting within the first ten minutes, even if it is only to agree with someone or to pitch in with some prepared comment or question:

---

[4]Brescoll, V. L. (2011). Who Takes the Floor and Why: Gender, Power, and Volubility in Organizations. *Administrative Science Quarterly*, *56*(4), 622-641.

Heath, K., & Holt, J. F. (2014, August 01). Women, Find Your Voice. Retrieved from https://hbr.org/2014/06/women-find-your-voice

'Could we look at it this way?'

'Is it possible to try this?'

This will soon become a habit and help others realize that you are invested in your career and your company. You will gradually garner respect, build up influence and attract new opportunities for advancement. Just come prepared to meetings with a few thoughts and talking points to help break the ice. Come a little early and sound the others out on what they are thinking. At the end, stay back for a few minutes, discuss issues and clarify responses so that the others feel you are part of the team. You may have noticed that men go at each other hammer and tongs at a meeting, but hang out together over a coffee or a drink afterwards. A casual conversation may often work wonders when negotiations seem to be failing.

Each person has a style of working and it is necessary to fine-tune it to achieve the best results. You may need to be more forthright, take more risks or seek out diverse skills and experiences as a means to get ahead. But that does not make you inferior to a colleague who is aggressive and needs to talk less. He can probably do with some lessons too! You may think that your high emotionality is a negative trait. You tend to get upset when someone criticizes you, and you get emotional and react hastily. Well, emotions, per se, are not negative. You just need to control them. Let yourself feel bad or angry and then quickly move on. Use your emotional strength to connect with people, find out how they are doing before making your pitch or plunging into shop talk. Make them see you as a friend and a partner.

Use your Emotional Quotient (EQ). Study your audience

and tailor your message suitably. If they appear to think you are coming on too strongly, tell them that you are being assertive in order to get the job done for the company. After all, that was why you were hired! You are merely using your strength to get better deals from your suppliers, higher prices from your customers and so on. If someone else takes credit for your work, go up to the person and tell them that it annoys you. They will think twice about doing this again. Do not confide your issues in a co-worker for often it comes back to hurt you.

When it is time for promotions and pay hikes, make sure that you put your best foot forward. Do not hesitate to negotiate for better pay or position, but be strategic about it. Be ready to list specific accomplishments that have helped enhance processes or improve profits. Frame it as something positive for the organization and not just for yourself.

'Pronouns matter,' according to Sheryl Sandberg, who advises women to say, '*We* had a great year' instead of '*I* had a great year'. She also advocates that you smile frequently, express appreciation and emphasize common interests. Negotiations can often be long drawn-out and you need to stay focused and resolute...and smile!

As *Fortune* magazine editor Pattie Sellers puts it, you should think of your career as a jungle gym, not as a ladder. As a woman, you are often unable to climb straight up as you need to take time off or work part-time, switch careers or work around barriers. A jungle gym, on the other hand, allows you to find more flexible, creative solutions, moving up, down or sideways to finally reach the top.

Set your goals for the short and the long term. Do you

want to reach the top, in say, ten years? Then choose a company that offers the maximum potential for fast growth. Do you want to have a creative job where you are your own boss? Look for fields such as writing or photography that offer you this. Do you want to put aside a nest egg so that you will have free time to do other things, like travelling or playing the drums? Plan your moves to make this possible. You could even freelance or work part-time, monetizing your passion for cooking or languages by offering classes at home.

Saying 'yes' or 'no'

This is probably the key decision that will make or break your career graph. A non-assertive person often finds it impossible to say 'no' and is soon overwhelmed by the results of her 'Yes-athon'! As Apple co-founder Steve Jobs put it, 'It's only by saying "no" that you can concentrate on the things that are really important.'

Let us first deal with situations where you may need to say 'yes'. As your advancement depends on satisfying your boss and/or key customers, you will often have to reprioritize your tasks in order to fulfil their requests. You may also consider doing someone a favour in the interest of building long-term relationships, especially if it will not take up much time or effort. Look for the opportunity hidden in the other person's request, for sometimes you may be able to pick up a new skill that will help in your personal or professional growth. Make sure, however, that you are the ideal person for the task and possess the right skills. If not, it would be better to point them in the direction of the best resources.

Moving on to saying 'no': This is essential when you

encounter harassment or abuse—physical, sexual or emotional. Do so at the very first occurrence so that things do not become worse. You must make your position clear and if you have to give up this job, so be it. You win some and lose some. If you do not handle it now, you will be unable to handle it when it recurs here or in another workplace. When it comes to work assignments, sometimes you may have to take time to weigh the consequences of saying 'no' to your bosses, against the cost of saying 'yes'. So, clearly explain your reasons for refusal. Perhaps you have other jobs that will be jeopardized if you take this up, or you do not have the right skills to do what they want. First, tell them that you appreciate the importance of the project they have assigned to you, and then explain the difficulties you may face. Offer indirect support if you can, for example, in some other area, or by freeing up someone from your team to help. Make sure that you do this face-to-face, so that it does not come across as insubordination or laziness.

If you need to say 'no' to a colleague, be straightforward in communicating this. If you try to be nice and say that you will try to find time, you are offering false hope and preventing your co-worker from getting the work done through someone else. Of course, you should be respectful by first listening carefully and then explaining your reasons, framing them in the context of serving the company's best interests. After saying 'no', do not feel guilty and say 'yes' blindly to the person's next request in order to compensate. Do not downplay your skills as a way to avoid doing something, because your colleagues may think that you are seeking reassurance or flattery. They may even use your words against you on some future occasion.

If you have to say 'no' to a junior, you should still be polite and help the person understand the reasons for your refusal. This is important in order to have a harmonious relationship and build an enthusiastic team. Allow the team members to give their reaction to your 'no', so that you can clear up any misunderstandings.

It is quite a challenging task to say 'no' to your customers, but in some situations you may have no other option. Allow them to have their say without interrupting, then repeat the key points so that they know you have listened carefully. Tell them how important they are to you and immediately offer them your best solution. Maybe you could say: 'Yes, we can do this once you have the premium package. This will also offer you other benefits.' This enables you to give a positive reply that will not endanger your relationship.

As you can see, the first step to advancement is *choosing* what you will or will not do. You will be better able to focus on your career when you free yourself from unnecessary baggage. These points apply to Mary, and also to Sheela, who is torn between her responsibilities at home and office.

2. CHANGE your working style

Make a start by listing three things you will begin to change this week. If a male co-worker keeps interrupting you or a female colleague, ask them to allow you or her to finish. Question their objection and force them to explain. Another option is to keep speaking and raise your voice too, if he raises his. Or call him out by saying, 'I'm not done yet. Can I have one more minute, please?' If he tries to make you out to be an emotional wreck, tell him clearly, 'I'm angry because you said/did this to mess up the project.' Shift the focus to the work, not to your perceived anger.

Completely ignore personal comments aimed at belittling you

There will always be boors who will judge you for looking too young, too old, too big, too pretty, or not pretty enough. Do not dignify them by taking notice. Also, never be apologetic, for then you will be looked upon as weaker and more blameworthy. You deserve your job just as much as anyone else. Heck, you may be better than the others and on your way to the top! Do not curl up into a ball, trying to protect yourself from aggression or ridicule. Do not be afraid to rock the boat as it is the other person who started the 'battle' by being unfair or abusive. Practise what to say to a habitual offender and then say it. Do not wait until things get out of hand and you explode over something trivial, playing into his hands. There is nothing wrong in standing up for yourself or getting angry when you feel insulted.

If you are a working mother like Sheela, you will often face rude questions or comments implying that you are neglecting your duties both at home and work. As it is, you are wrestling with your own guilt, trying to be in two places at once and questioning your choices. Decide now on how many hours a day you are willing to work and how much work-based travel you are willing to undertake, if required. Reassess your decision and amend it if necessary. If this does not work out later, you will at least know that you did everything you could to make it work on your own terms.

You may be criticized as someone who is trying to 'have it all', whereas the reality may be that you are a single mother, or the primary breadwinner and your focus is on 'not losing it all'. You may have no alternative to juggling responsibilities and trying not to fail as a parent or an employee. It doesn't help that society believes that men can enjoy both a rewarding career and a happy home life, whereas for a woman, it is regarded as difficult, if not impossible.

If you run away from conflict in order to keep the peace, you start a war within yourself. Practise expressing your opinion clearly and confronting issues head-on, using 'I'-based statements. Keep moving forward, avoiding the inclination to backpedal. For women who have to grapple with their role as mother and wife, go back to the previous chapter and implement the steps described. Always ask for what you need. Give yourself permission to gracefully accept compliments for your work. Say 'thank you' and take credit.

3. Five steps to CREATE a new 'you'

It is time to begin celebrating the person you are. Here are five macro-level steps to awaken the goddess within you.

- Put yourself first and before others, and address issues directly instead of waiting for them to overwhelm you. You are not being selfish, just smart. Remember, a confident 'you' translates into a harmonious family and a pleasant work environment. You were the one who gave too much. The good thing is that you are the one who can change it too.
- Say 'no' to people and actions that drain you. Surround yourself with positive people and relationships that energize you and encourage you to be your best. Ask

for their help while you make the change.

- Invest in your financial health so that you are never a victim, at the mercy of a bully or adverse circumstances. Safeguard physical health, fuelling your body with exercise and healthy foods instead of cakes and cookies.

- Feed the inner you. Your mantra may be spirituality, religion or compassion. The tools you use may vary, ranging from prayer, yoga and meditation, to nature, music and social service. You cannot ignore your soul when you are grappling everyday with spiritual decline, cynicism and despair. You need a moral compass and something to make your spirit soar: beauty, love, courage, wonder... Connect to your inner self and create a personal practice that will help you attain higher levels of well-being.

- You may not be perfect but you still have the right to happiness and respect. Do not second-guess yourself, questioning your action or inaction in the past. You had your reasons then and you chose the best option available to you at that point. Make your decision now to strengthen yourself, to be honest about your needs, and to be courageous and ambitious.

These steps can be used profitably by everyone—even men who are timid or reserved; or those who face disrespect due to their class or background. Always remember that you are unique and that you deserve to be respected. Be bold, be original. Use your voice for yourself and for others. Success awaits you!

Tip: *Keep a journal to record your achievements over the last year. Browse through it whenever you feel low or wish to prepare yourself to ask for a promotion. And here's a bonus tip: Apply for that higher-level post even if you do not have all the skills specified. Your enthusiasm may well tip the balance in your favour.*

Let us now look at the story of Indrani, wife of the king of the heavens, Indra. Discover how she outwitted a lecher with aplomb!

Indrani: Outsmarting a Lecherous King

Once, the asura Vritra, who was made invincible by Brahma's boons, tyrannized earth and drove Indra from his throne in the heavens. Both worlds were lost in darkness and anarchy and the devas prayed to Shakti to help them. Meanwhile, the rishis went to Vritra and urged him to make friends with Indra so that harmony would prevail. The asura sought an assurance from Indra and the devas that they would not kill him during the day or night, with any weapon—solid or liquid, or of fire or light. When Indra swore to this, the asura embraced him as a friend. However, wily Indra was merely waiting patiently to strike. At twilight one day, Indra summoned his thunderbolt, into which Vishnu entered, changing it into a weapon of foam. The celestial king invoked Shakti and used the weapon of foam to kill the asura. Vritra stared at him in dismay as he fell, shocked at the treachery from one he had believed to be his friend. The asura's father Vishvakarma cursed Indra for his betrayal. Indra lost all his strength and fled from Amaravati, leaving behind his throne and his queen. He turned himself into a water snake and hid in the stalk of a huge lotus that grew in Lake Manasarovar.

When the devas failed to find their king after a long search, they decided to look for another king to govern the realms. They chose Nahusha, the son of Aayu, a king of the lunar dynasty. Nahusha was learned, generous and skilled in the Vedas and in weaponry. 'You are valorous like Surya, brilliant like Agni and charitable like Kubera. Come and be our king,' the gods said to Nahusha. He accepted the throne and ruled wisely for a long period. However, power and success gradually corrupted him and he became lustful and arrogant. He saw Indrani, Indra's wife, one day and was captivated by her beauty. He began to spend every day and night lusting for her.

Nahusha summoned the devas and told them that he was now the new 'Indra' and Indrani belonged to him. 'Make her come to my bed at once,' he commanded. The devas tried to advise Nahusha, telling him that Indrani could not marry another while Indra was still alive. However, Nahusha grew enraged and refused to listen. 'Go to her and convince her with sweet words, or bring her to me by force. You will face my wrath if you do not do as I say!'

The devas and their guru Brihaspati went to Indrani's palace to convey Nahusha's command. Brihaspati was afraid of the King and tried to persuade Indrani to join the new king in his bed. 'Indra fled from Amaravati, giving up his position and all his belongings,' he said. 'Hence, you should go to Nahusha, who is the new "Indra".'

Indrani's eyes burned with wrath. 'I am not a possession to be handed over to another man!' she said. 'I am still Indra's wife and will not give that up for anything. You may be afraid but I am not. I am dismayed that you should even suggest something so shameless. I look into the future and see that it is your wife Tara who will behave in the manner you suggest today, deserting you for another man.' (And so it happened, when, for a time, Tara lived with the Moon God and had a son by him.)

Indra's queen chastised the devas as well for bringing her this shameful message. 'Have you forgotten that Indra lost his strength and went into hiding only because he killed the asura that tyrannized you all? Show him your loyalty or I will curse you all!'

The devas stood with their heads bowed as she pondered over the next course of action. 'I will go to Nahusha and speak to him. His brain is addled by desire and prompts him to act rashly. I will contrive a way to rescue all of us from this dilemma.'

The devas rushed to Nahusha and told him that Indrani was coming to see him. The lustful king was delighted and put on his most ornate robes and jewels in preparation. He sat proudly on his throne, telling himself that the queen was coming to him because she was enthralled by his power and splendour. 'I will make her apologize later for her delay in coming to me—but later...much later...after I have tasted her charms in my bed,' he thought.

Indrani came before him, looked at his proud face and demeanour, and cursed him in her heart. She decided to stand her ground bravely even if he ordered his men to seize her. But first, she would befuddle him with her charm. She assumed a respectful manner and spoke to him in a sweet voice. 'My respects to you, Lord of Amaravati!' she said.

'Welcome, fair one!' he said in reply, his eyes alight with desire. 'I am delighted that you have come to pay obeisance to the lord of the heavens. Accept me now as your husband and join me on the throne and in my bed.'

Hearing his distasteful words, Indrani trembled for a moment but then stiffened her resolve. 'Wise king, lord of the devas!' she said. 'Pray, grant me a boon that will enable me to come to you with a clear conscience and a loving heart. Allow me to find out first if Indra is dead or alive. Once I determine that he has indeed perished, I will happily come to you to rule by your side.'

Nahusha thought for a moment and then nodded. 'Do so quickly, my beloved. I will be eagerly waiting for your return,' he said.

She flashed a seductive smile at him before she left, and Nahusha was convinced that she was dazzled by his magnificence and power.

Indrani returned to her palace where she worshipped Shakti. The goddess transported her in one swift moment to the shores of the Manasarovar. At once, Indra, who had been performing penances to reclaim his throne, emerged from the water as a snake and resumed his natural form so that he could take her in his arms. They wept to see each other after such a long absence and he remarked that she had grown gaunt in his absence. 'Then return with me to Amaravati, O Indra, before I should die from anguish,' she said. 'King Nahusha, who rules in your place, torments us all and lusts for your queen. He threatens me and the devas with dire consequences if I will not share his bed. I will kill him or die in the attempt, rather than allow him to lay a finger on me. But before taking such a harsh course, I wanted to come to you and reveal all that has transpired. Beloved Indra, you are the only one who can defeat him and reinstate dharma. Come with me to our capital and overthrow the upstart.'

'Dearest heart, I cannot come with you now,' Indra replied. 'I am yet to complete my penances for abusing Vritra's friendship. Also, I have still not fully recovered my strength to be able to fight Nahusha. However, do not fear, my love. The devas and the Trimurti know that you are peerless and devoted to me. But I know something more—that you are wise and inventive and need no one's help to save yourself. Use your wit to find a way out of this quandary. I know you can.' So saying, he turned into a snake again and slid into the lotus stalk to continue his austerities.

Indrani returned to Nahusha and told him, 'I have looked everywhere but have not been able to find my husband. I will gladly become your queen now if you should satisfy a desire of mine that not even Indra could. Can you promise to do that?'

Nahusha was excited at the idea of marrying Indrani and hastily promised to fulfil her wish. 'All the gods have exalted vehicles,' she said. 'Shiva has Nandi and Vishnu has Garuda. Even Surya, who is your subject, has a chariot drawn by celestial horses. As the lord of devaloka, should you not have a vehicle that surpasses all these, something that no one has seen before?'

'What is this vehicle you speak of, Indrani? Tell me at once!' said Nahusha.

'Come to me on a palanquin carried by the great rishis. Let the world see that no one is greater than you, bold Nahusha. If you are able to do this, I will accept your proposal gladly.'

'Your creative genius surpasses even your beauty,' he replied. 'Do not doubt that I will carry out your wish. No man or god—least of all an ascetic—can refuse my command. I shall come to you in splendour on a palanquin borne by the rishis.'

Indrani returned to her palace while he summoned the sages and ordered them to bear his golden palanquin. The three worlds trembled, for it was a sacrilege to employ the sages in this fashion. However, the rishis agreed to do so, out of the generosity of their hearts, but found it difficult to carry his weight in the palanquin. They struggled forward, one step at a time, while Nahusha stirred impatiently, intoxicated by thoughts of taking Indrani in his arms. They finally came within sight of Indrani's palace and the king saw her waiting on her balcony. His excitement mounted and he grew dizzy with desire. He lashed out furiously with his foot at one of the rishis before him. 'Sarpa, sarpa!' he exclaimed, which meant 'go faster'. The one he so abused was the illustrious Sage Agastya, with such wondrous powers that he had once swallowed the whole ocean in one gulp. The lustful Nahusha had forgotten all decorum in his eagerness to show Indrani that he was more powerful than her previous husband. Agastya, who had been staggering under the weight on his shoulders, was shocked, and stopped in his tracks. 'Sarpa!' shouted Nahusha, kicking him again.

'Sarpa? May you become a sarpa!' cursed Agastya. And the king instantly turned into a serpent, for that was another meaning of the word. Nahusha's lust and insolence had paved the way to his doom. 'Foul king, fall to the earth and spend the rest of your life crawling on your belly and eating rodents as food,' the sage roared, his eyes flaming.

Nahusha realized how grievously he had sinned. He looked down at his body, now glinting with serpentine scales. 'Great sage! Forgive a sinner whose senses were disordered by lust,' he cried out in anguish, his voice emerging as a snake's hiss. 'Take back your curse, I beseech you,' he screamed as he tumbled headlong towards the distant earth.

'A rishi's curse cannot be withdrawn,' Agastya replied. 'You will pay for your sin by suffering for thousands of years. Finally, the Pandava, Yudhishthira, will redeem you, after enlightening you on dharma and kingship.'

Indrani rejoiced at having felled the lecherous king with her masterstroke. The devas praised her ingenuity and hurried to bring Indra back to his palace. Indra had completed his tapasya by then, and returned to his throne. He praised his queen wholeheartedly for being as intelligent as she was bewitching. The realms returned to harmony again. The fires of the sages burned bright and rain blessed the earth in the right season. The planets shone brilliantly in the sky and the lofty mountains yielded rich stores of gems. The devas rejoiced under the rule of their glorious queen and her consort.

LESSONS LEARNED

In some versions of the tale, Indrani is shown weeping and seeking the help of Brihaspati and the devas. She bewails her fate that Indra should have left her to face the lecherous Nahusha all alone. However, in the *Skanda Purana*, we see her as a quick-thinking and enterprising queen who comes up with a plan to destroy the lustful king whom even the devas are afraid to oppose. She curses Brihaspati, who seeks to sway her and make her give up her principles in order to survive. She stresses on the dharma that the devas should follow, and chastises them for asking her to sacrifice herself to Nahusha's lust.

Do you now perceive Indrani as a great model to follow in a world where men rule the roost and often prey on women? Like her, you too must stand up for your rights, and use your wit and willpower to attain your goals. In no way are women inferior to men in intelligence or capacity. All the barriers you face will fall when you act like Indrani—resourceful, focused and creative.

5
Young, Not Oppressed

Sushma is sixteen years old, smart as a whip and dreams of a career in medicine. But her parents are already looking for a suitable groom in order to get her married as soon as she graduates. How can she convince them that this is not what she wants, that this is not the life she wishes to lead? Moreover, how can she accept a life with a stranger when her own thoughts on marriage are unformed?

Anita is twenty years old and was married off the previous year to a software engineer who works in another city. She had been planning to do her post-graduation but was instead forced to 'settle down' and become a mother the very next year. A life in her husband's shadow—is that all that life holds for her? She would like to work, but who will give her a job and who will do the babysitting?

If you are just entering your twenties or even your thirties, you are faced with many issues that seem impossible to overcome. As a young woman in India, you find that your freedom is limited in many ways by the people around you. You may be studying, you may or may not be in a relationship, you may be married and perhaps also a mother, or you may be working towards building your career—whatever your situation, this book will help you choose a meaningful life where you are valued for your unique personality and abilities.

If you have just graduated, you are filled with a sense of achievement and joy. You imagine that the world and all its opportunities are spread out at your feet. You are free to shape your future in any way you wish. However, with freedom of choice comes uncertainty. In which direction should you proceed? What do you want your future to be?

Before rushing to follow the herd, you should spend time discovering yourself—your personality traits, strengths and weaknesses. Then you must start honing your skills and come up with an action plan. Do not choose a course of study just because others say that it is the way to get a big salary. Do not take up a job offer if you think that the work will be monotonous or exhausting. Remember that you will be working for some forty years before you retire and that you do not want to be stuck doing something you hate. Of course, there are always people around you who will second-guess your choices, telling you that you should do this or that. But whose life is it anyway?

WHERE FEAR RULES THE MIND

There are definitely more opportunities opening up for young girls and women today, as you have greater access to education and professions. But discrimination is also deep-rooted in a culture where a girl child is often regarded as a burden. As a girl, you may be more rigidly controlled than your brother/male cousin, and forced to fit into roles that society has determined for you. You may find that you are unconsciously adapting to expectations from others, changing from the bright, cheerful girl you were, into a diffident adolescent. You are compelled to fit in with peers, with parental beliefs, and with society's vision of how you should be. You are told that you must look good, maintain an ideal weight, learn skills such as cooking and housekeeping, and prioritize marriage over a career. When you assert yourself, saying that you want to create your own identity, you are called troublesome and misguided. Even movies sometimes portray working women as being harried and unhappy and you begin to believe that this may be your fate, too.

Your parents often focus on saving for your marriage rather than spending on your education. They may think that anything you earn will anyway profit only your husband's family. Money may not be the hurdle in other cases. Your parents may genuinely be afraid for your safety, especially if further studies involve living away from home. There is also a lurking fear that you may come across unsuitable men and form an attachment. Frequent news reports of sexual violence against women also tilts the balance against you at a time when you are already under stress, trying to create your own identity, seeking a job or financial independence.

Often, it is implied that girls are a burden to be handed over to someone else. Marriage is a transfer of rights where the right to control you is passed on to another family who gets to decide every aspect of your life. Your husband and his family will now tell you what to wear, whether to work, who you will meet, and even control your access to your family and friends. They will seek to impose their own values, attitudes and behaviours on you. An independent woman is regarded as a threat to society, as being spoiled or too modern—just the opposite of the ideal woman they have in mind. Some of the old thinking that regarded women as 'dumb' or 'helpless' is now being replaced by new biases that seek to determine the boundaries of a woman's empowerment.

YOU DON'T HAVE TO BE SUPERWOMAN

You may somehow manage to continue in a job after marriage. But it is a daily struggle to match new expectations with old responsibilities, and you push yourself into a corner trying to be Superwoman. You read up articles on multitasking. You buy ready-to-eat dinners and feel guilty that you are not cooking from scratch. You check official emails on your phone as you wait for the milk to boil. You try to plan your grocery shopping for maximum efficiency and almost kill yourself bringing in the heavy bags and finding space in your refrigerator. Nevertheless, you run out of bread or eggs and are forced to go out again in the middle of the week. You try to prove to your family and yourself that you can dish up a three-course meal after a long day at work, or get up at midnight to check your child's temperature when she has a cough. What happens if you have to take leave to take her to the doctor when you know that appraisals are due at work? And there is your husband, maybe watching a cricket match on TV—his life as smooth as always, not realizing that you are in dire need of help.

The truth is that there are only twenty-four hours in a day and that you cannot be in two places at the same time—at work and at home. There is no point in subjecting yourself to depression or anxiety attacks, or lashing out at your husband instead of asking him for specific help.

Maybe you think that you will never have these problems and that you will not allow yourself to reach such a state. After all, you are educated and have a job as well. Perhaps your family is rich and can take care of all your material needs. You have nothing to worry about. Life is meant for shopping, enjoying a comfortable life and moving on to married life in another well-to-do family that takes over the responsibility to provide for you. So why rock the boat? Why get the reputation of being difficult?

However, have you considered whether this situation will be permanent? What if life is not always so smooth? How many women have been caught unawares when they find that marriage is not all love and kisses, or when they lose their husband to death or divorce? There is no way you can handle a crisis if you are unprepared. Isn't it safer to be able to rely on yourself and not on someone else?

It is always better to ensure that your rights are respected; for often, what is readily granted to men is out of reach for women. Here are some scenarios where you may need to speak up for yourself:

1. Free to study or to work

As a youngster, you are filled with energy, ambition and the desire to attain your dreams. You are also under a great deal of pressure stemming from your own expectations and those of others. You worry about many things—being attractive, being liked, and wondering if you are too fat or too thin. You are in constant competition with your peers, and have to deal with uncertain relationships and mood swings. Family and friends do not respect your personal space, and random strangers target you with unwanted advances. Your parents start insisting that you should not stay out late and that you should avoid spending time with male friends. You feel unsafe in public spaces and wonder if you need to learn some form of martial arts to protect yourself. If you are from a small town or a rural area, you have fewer opportunities for higher studies or a career and are doubtful about your communication skills. Added to this is your diffidence in pursuing your goal, to even ask your lecturer for a recommendation letter to apply for higher studies. How do you convince your parents that you may need to live in a hostel to study further? How do you make them understand that marriage should come only after you are self-reliant? Or that you are looking for other things in a marriage than your mother did? How do we apply the three Cs to your life? Keep reading and we will discuss all that.

2. Free to marry or not

Falling in love and being in a relationship are wonderful experiences, but can also be painful and stressful. You are on a high one moment, only to be brought down by a sudden turn of events, a misunderstanding or even an unanswered phone call. You are ripped apart by bursts of jealousy, anger, loneliness and insecurity. You face failure and rejection every day and make choices blindly, without knowing if they are the right ones for you.

Even as you struggle with internal conflicts, you face maximum pressure from your family to get married to someone of their choice, someone who meets their criteria of caste, community and class. Maybe you wish to equip yourself with professional skills or take up a job to be financially independent. But your parents tell you that being single after a certain age is not good and that the best bridegrooms will be snatched away by others. You will not be able to have children if you delay too long and they themselves are getting old and want to complete their responsibilities. They resort to emotional blackmail, telling you that they are eager to see their grandchildren. They are also afraid of what people will say if you remain single. Relatives will wonder if there's something wrong with you or say that your parents are irresponsible. Faced with so many arguments, you are likely to throw up your hands in despair. It takes immense patience to deal with all this. But always remember that you have the right to be happy. Stay firm until you are ready to take the step yourself and with the right man.

3. Free to decide on relationships

Women's status in India is still so dismal that the Supreme Court has been forced to declare as recently as April 2017 that a woman has the right to love or to reject someone's advances.[5] Her individual choice is legally recognized and

[5]Sinha, B. (2017, April 28). Woman has a right to love and live, man must not ignore civility: SC. Retrieved from https://www.hindustantimes. com/india-news/woman-has-a-right-to-love-and-live-man-must-not-ignore-civility-sc/story-qmSfPwBzvZdrY4sUhnJlsM.html

has to be socially respected. Male chauvinism has no role to play in her life. The judges asked in anguish, why women are not allowed to live in peace, and to enjoy dignity and freedom. In this case, a man was convicted of abetting a girl's suicide through his continuous harassment. Society gives this disgusting practice the bland label of 'eve-teasing', in itself a bid to downplay the seriousness of the offence.

Sadly, a girl in our country is at risk of 'honour' killing if she goes against society's diktats in choosing her husband. She may be attacked with acid or stabbed if she rejects a stalker's advances.

After marriage, her freedom may be restricted as she is confined to the house and is subjected to excessive pressure to produce a male child. Added to these, she faces risks such as dowry harassment, domestic or workplace violence, and poor safety when she leaves the house.

How can we apply the three Cs to these scenarios?

CHOOSE YOUR COURSE IN LIFE

The following are some pointers if your battle is with parents about marriage or a career.

As an empowered woman, you know what you want—to be married, have a family, or have a successful career. You also know the path you need to take to achieve your dream. If you want to get married, then you must date with that goal in mind. If it is about career, then you should work towards getting that promotion or starting that company. Are you going after what you want?

The first step to being empowered is to be comfortable

with who you are and being confident that you can face any situation on your own. It doesn't matter whether you have a partner or not—in business or life. Being happy with your own personality energizes you in many ways. If you do have a partner, even then you need to ensure that he/she does not stop you from doing what you want to do. Treat yourself to a movie or a weekend getaway. Make it a goal to try something new that you wouldn't normally do alone. 'If you obey all the rules, you miss all the fun,' said actress Katharine Hepburn. Have a sense of humour, pick yourself up after a failure and get going again. As the wise novelist Anaïs Nin, puts it: 'Life shrinks or expands in proportion to one's courage.'

Maybe your mother was married at seventeen and had two kids by the time she was twenty-one. This does not mean that you have to as well. You do not have to rush to pick out your man in the 'marriage market' before 'stocks run out'! Being single no longer has negative connotations. Instead, a single woman is viewed increasingly as someone who is free, empowered and intelligent. So, push relentlessly for higher education, at the end of which you can apply for jobs. You could even take up a part-time job if you need to find money to study further, perhaps through evening courses or distance education. If you get a good job in a different city, it would divert your parents' focus from your single status to your safety and prospects at work! Having a job and living away from home gives you more confidence and shows your family that you are capable of handling things on your own. You are financially independent and are able to put forth your opinions more effectively. Seeing that you are more vocal, your parents too will look for grooms in a different way. They will look for more liberal households that will foster or, at least, not hinder your independence.

To make this possible, you may need to seek the help of an elder brother or sister, or an enlightened relative who will see things from your point of view and support your stance. Be calm and reasonable, give logical examples and explanations to advance your case, and remember always that this is your life and you need to have a say in deciding what you will or will not do. Set aside your fears about taking matters into your own hands, as most problems you anticipate may not materialize. And even if they do, you can use the skills you have developed to take them on and emerge stronger.

CHANGE THE WAY YOU LOOK AT RELATIONSHIPS

When you decide that you are ready for marriage, you have probably had a taste of independence, perhaps through living in a hostel or going to work. You are more knowledgeable about the outside world and have your own expectations from your partner and married life. Love, companionship and respect are as important to you now as financial security. You want your husband to share your dreams, to support you in case of problems with in-laws and to allow you freedom to retain your identity after marriage as well. After all, given that you are smart and independent in your professional life, why become a slave at home?

Now comes the big question of arranged or love marriage. Both have pluses and minuses and perhaps equal chances of being successful. In an arranged marriage, you have the advantage of family support that may come in useful when you have children or when you face problems with your husband or in-laws. In a love marriage, the onus is on you to choose the right person and then work with him to make the marriage a success. Even in an arranged marriage, you should insist on your criteria being met as far as possible. It is essential that you are able to respect your partner in order to make it work. So, screen the matrimonial requests your parents receive or send out. Also, ensure that you are able to interact with the man several times until you are satisfied that you will be happy if you marry him.

You may find it difficult to find the right man to marry, though there are many matrimonial or dating sites where men declare their intent to enter into a long-term relationship. Some young men today suffer from the 'Peter Pan Syndrome'—an inability to grow up. Life, to them, is an endless round of enjoyment without commitment. They are focused on having a good time, which translates into drinking, watching sports programmes with buddies, and dating a series of women. A person who is so self-centred may not make a good husband or father, for his values are those of a culture that idolizes youth, beauty and pleasure above responsibilities.

So, have a meaningful discussion with your date on issues that matter—not just on movies, fashion or lifestyle. Do not be shy or think that it is not 'feminine' to ask difficult questions before marriage, for you need to have the answers if you wish to have a stable married life.

A key subject to discuss is that of having children—how many and when, and whether he will share the responsibility and help change diapers, for instance. How important is religion? This becomes crucial if you are from different backgrounds. Often, conflict arises when you have children and the question of bringing them up in a particular faith arises. You need to assign responsibilities in earning, spending and saving for the future. What are your career goals? Will household duties be shared or does he have a woman-only attitude? Also, what are both your views on earlier relationships? Will he be jealous or judgemental? Can you both let go of the past as long as it remains in the past? Remember that there is no correct answer to these questions except what both of you are comfortable with. Also, you do not have to get into all this in the first meeting, but if matters are getting serious, you should begin to delve into issues that could make or break a marriage. Better before than after, right?

CREATE A HAPPY 'YOU'

What defines a great relationship? It consists of two independent people who acknowledge and cherish each other and are ready to depend on each other. Traditionally, this has been a one-way street, with the woman brought up from childhood to look up to men. You must realize that when you are his equal, you can add a lot of value to the marriage. When you are independent, you have your own routine and priorities. These could be education, work or social commitments that allow you to be yourself and also give your partner time to spend on his interests. When you come together after indulging in your individual pursuits, you are more focused on each other and your relationship is more vibrant, because you can engage with the other on many levels. You are more interesting and bring more 'spice' to the relationship. Your expectations are also more realistic, rather than being based on colourful rom-com movies!

Start off your life the way you want it to go on. Say 'yes' to small things while being firm on big ones that threaten your dignity. Remember that you are part of a family and must do your part in keeping things running. Respect your partner just as you expect to be respected. Learning basic domestic skills will help you survive if your maid suddenly takes leave, as pizza or instant food thrice a day will soon lose its charm! Maybe you can please your in-laws by wearing traditional clothes on festive occasions while wearing modern outfits to work. Learn to deal calmly with your in-laws and resolve things yourself, without dragging your husband into the argument. You earn respect this way and also show that you are not a pushover. Share your likes and dislikes and your dreams with him, and ask him to share his own. This will make your marriage stronger and more fulfilling. Discuss contraceptive options so that when you do have children, it will be when both of you are ready for the responsibility. Learn about finances, saving money and filing tax returns, whether you are working or not. Remember, you are an equal partner; you share responsibilities and may even have to take over in a crisis. Speak up if you disagree on something and do not succumb to emotional blackmail or a desire to please everyone.

Keep your options open. Be healthy, fit and self-reliant. Build a network of supportive people. Get rid of fears that hold you back. Never stop learning. Freeing and expanding your mind is an important step towards empowering yourself, so educate yourself in *any* way you can. Even if you don't have a formal education, there are still plenty of ways to increase your knowledge. Taking the initiative to teach yourself something new is one of the most empowering things you can do. Read books, go to the library or a bookstore, join a book club, or research on the Internet. Why not sign up for a class that interests you? It can be as simple as knitting or as complex as physics. The point is to explore an area you have never explored before. Look for weekend workshops in your newspaper, or drop by your local institutes to see what classes they have to offer. And if you are a busy mom with no time to take a class, check out an educational book from the library and read a few pages before going to bed each night. A smart woman is an empowered woman. No one dares mess with her! Aim to be a strong individual and an equal partner. Everyone in a family profits when both partners have careers. Sharing financial and household responsibilities leads to happier mothers, more involved fathers and resourceful children. When you play multiple roles, you will be less anxious, more settled, enjoy greater emotional and financial security, and lead a more satisfying life. Go for it!

Tip: *Nothing cures anxiety like action. You will find that you spend more energy avoiding things than actually doing them! Completing a task makes you feel clever and accomplished, and elevates your mood. 'Doing' produces results, and reveals more things to be done. So, get going and reach out for change, success, creativity, health and happiness.*

Now, let's read a story portraying the ultimate equality between the sexes—the story of Shiva and Parvati fused into one!

Ardhanarishwara: Being Equal

Sati may have prayed ceaselessly to attain Shiva, but it is he who comes to her when she is reborn as Parvati and then seeks out her father Himavan, in order to marry her. This is a role reversal of sorts, indicating that the two are equal in power and that each is incomplete without the other. While the early puranas show Shakti being created from the gods, the later ones depict her as the Supreme One, who creates gods, men and asuras.

How did the divine couple achieve a balance of power, and how did she become half of his body? Let us take a peek into their lives, shall we?

Shiva made changes in his appearance and behaviour in order to please his beloved and to placate Mena, Parvati's mother, who was alarmed by his fierce form. He turned his matted locks into an orderly coiffure and transformed his serpents into golden chains. The fearful third eye became a sparkling gem adorning his forehead. The ash that normally covered his body, became fragrant sandalwood paste. He wore a gold diadem instead of his garland of skulls, and Vishnu came to help adorn him in such a way that Parvati would find her groom even more attractive than Kama. Parvati had worn robes of bark and shed her royal clothes and jewels in order to perform tapasya to win the ascetic Shiva. This time, he made amends for his delay in accepting her by bringing fragrances, silks and ornaments to adorn the princess who was now the queen of his heart.

Like all newly-married couples, Shiva and Parvati also had their differences. When she pointed out that he had no house on Mount Kailasa for them to live in, he replied that he was an ascetic and did not need one.

'Do we not need a roof to protect us from the hot winds and sun?' she asked.

'Not when our abode is itself the roof of the world!' he countered.

When she persisted, however, he fulfilled her desire in his own way. 'We will find shelter in the shade of the trees,' he said as he led her into the moonlit forest. Then came the monsoon, when the skies grew dark with thunderclouds. 'How will I live in the open when lightning and rain threaten my peace?' she asked him. 'We will stay above the clouds so the rains cannot touch us,' he said and flew with her to the top of the highest cloud. She loved the way he cherished her, and admired his power over the elements. Everything was an adventure as romance was in the air. But the problem had merely been shelved, not solved!

Gradually, Parvati transformed Kailasa into a beautiful home and Shiva into a caring householder. The mountain cave became her palace and the mountain slopes her lawns. The two courted each other on snowy peaks and near forest pools, amidst golden deer and gleaming swans. She was gentle and graceful while he was rough and exuberant. He was the guru who taught her the sacred scriptures and the mystic texts. She was also his teacher, directing his awareness to worldly concerns. Her incisive questions on good and evil, birth and death, and suffering and salvation, were answered by Shiva, to be passed on to humanity through the sages. Bewitched by her intellect and her intuition, Shiva proclaimed to the world that man should henceforth offer worship or sacrifice only with his wife by his side. She was the body to his spirit, the mind to his soul, and Prakriti to his Purusha.

But their quarrels did not end, provoked at times by the sages who were jealous of Parvati and her proximity to their previously ascetic god. Once, Sage Bhringi angered Parvati by ignoring her and going around Shiva alone, chanting prayers. She moved closer to Shiva so that there was no gap between them, but the sage took the form of a bee and went round Shiva's topknot. Shiva then made her half of himself, taking the form of Ardhanarishwara, half man and half woman. But the stubborn Bhringi took the form of a worm and tried to burrow between them.

'Foolish Bhringi!' said Parvati. 'You seek to shun Shakti, forgetting that your flesh and blood come from her. Suffer now for your sins by becoming devoid of flesh.' The curse took effect at once. The sage became a bag of bones and collapsed on the floor, unable to stand up. He begged for her forgiveness and she gave him a third leg to balance himself. However, she ordained that he would remain like this forever, teaching the world an important lesson that Shiva and Shakti together make a whole and that neither can exist without the other. Parvati was now happy in Shiva's love and there was no more bickering, as there was no separation. This was the ultimate union—of worshipper with god, of desire with release.

However, the world became barren as the two were fused into one. The two halves had to separate so that new life could blossom through procreation. And when they became two, their bickering began again, adding spice to their lives and making their reunion more blissful.

After one such quarrel with Parvati, Shiva left in a huff to resume his austerities in the forest, considering that it would be better to avoid all the turmoil of married life. Parvati grew lonely without him and decided to woo him back. She took the form of Shabari, a huntress, and went to him, dressed in colourful robes and beads, with peacock feathers in her hair and a song on her lips. So beautiful was she that even the bees in the forest were overcome with desire. When her dancing steps and lively song disturbed Shiva's meditation, he opened his eyes and fell victim to desire. 'Who are you, lovely one, and what do you seek here?' he asked her. She looked at him coquettishly from under lowered eyelids and told him that she was looking for a husband: 'One who is omniscient, who is lord of the realms and is able to fulfil all my needs!'

'I am the one you are looking for,' he said, but she shook her head. 'I know that you are married and that you deserted your wife, who attained you after fervent prayers,' she said.

'Nevertheless, I want you,' he exclaimed eagerly. 'I'll bring you beautiful skirts and silken blouses. I'll have the sun and the moon rise at your command and Indra stand guard at your doors. Do not worry about Parvati, who flouted my wishes, for I'll send her home to her father and make you my queen.'

The goddess smiled and directed him to her father to seek his permission to wed her. The besotted Shiva did so, only to realize that it was Himavan, who asked if Shiva was teasing him, for he was already married to his daughter. Realizing that his wife had lured him into love once again, Shiva retreated angrily to a remote corner of the universe. The lovelorn Parvati praised him lavishly so that he would be mollified. Shiva finally came back to be united with her again in a frenzy of love that rocked heaven and earth.

Parvati's praise of the God of Kailasa is nothing but the effusion of bhakti that wins over the gods. It is through these games that the divine couple showed devotees the true path to bliss.

The goddess took various forms to suit the occasion. When she had taken birth as Daksha's daughter Sati, and Shiva advised her not to attend her father's yagna uninvited, her anger at being curbed led to the birth of the Mahavidyas. These were terrifying forms of Shakti who mocked the submissive roles played by females and also the popular notion that a wife must obey her husband. Seeing Sati's fury, Shiva closed his eyes. When he opened them, fearsome Kali stood before him with dishevelled hair, lolling tongue and fiery eyes. She was black, which indicated not the absence of colour but the absorption of all colour. She embodied the power that drew the whole universe into itself and then emanated new life once more. She encircled him with her ten terrifying forms and he was forced to let her go. Later, when Daksha insulted Sati and Shiva, Kali destroyed him and his attendants with relish, showing the world what happens when a woman is scorned or abused. Also remember, that during Navaratri, we worship the Navadurgas, when the goddess manifests into nine forms that embody female independence and power.

LESSONS LEARNED

There are so many aspects and dimensions to love and passion, conflict and conciliation. It may be easy to enter into a physical relationship, but establishing an emotional union requires time and hard work. When two strong people come together, bringing with them their own ideas and ideals, fiery altercations are to be expected. Like Parvati, you too need to hold your own, retaining your own convictions and creativity. You need to reinvent yourself in many forms and play many roles—always remaining true to your inner self.

Parvati presents herself in many avatars, ranging from the gentle Gauri to the fearsome Kali. The midpoint is Durga, where she manifests her powers to optimum effect. She is absolute love and also absolute power—just as you can be. You too must work towards reaching the right point in the continuum. You may be born a 'Gauri', but may need to change in response to circumstances and people. You will need to enhance your capacity for love without sacrificing your individuality or independence. Like Durga, you need to be both soft and strong, forceful without being aggressive and loving without being submissive. It is no longer considered a masculine quality to have a drive to excel, so do not hold back from being ambitious at work. Focus on using your emotional intelligence to advance in your career, staying in touch with your heart while you work with your mind. You can do anything you wish to, and that includes being forceful yet caring, powerful yet passionate.

6
Reclaim Yourself and Your World

You have come a long way already, so first pat yourself on the back before continuing! You have seen how important it is to be looked at as a person—not just as a mother, wife, daughter, or working woman. You have acknowledged your desires and ambitions, and recognized the obstacles holding you back—insecurity, habit, diffidence, procrastination, or avoiding responsibility. You have also realized that no one else knows your mind or abilities better than you do. Your insights are more valuable than that of any scientist, as science is really just common sense at its best!

You have learned the difference between passive, aggressive and assertive behaviour. You may have realized that when you are submissive, you appear weak and give up control of your life. On the other hand, when you are aggressive, you feel angry and alone; others avoid you and call you obnoxious. Being assertive, however, yields positive results. You feel good about yourself and others respect you as a capable individual who stands up for her rights. You are able to express your feelings freely and accept credit for your accomplishments. You can voice complaints, criticism and disagreement when needed; not waiting until you are close to an explosion. You have begun to say 'no' to actions, people or situations that have previously sucked out all your energy and willpower.

Of course, you may feel that all this is really hard work. It may be easier to allow someone else to take care of you, to make excuses for yourself by saying that you are not bold or smart enough. You can become philosophical and say that this is your fate and you deserve to suffer. Once you realize how your own mind is working against you, it becomes easier to develop a plan of attack to handle this as well as the external issues you face. Remember that change is stressful in the short run as you have to create new patterns of behaviour. But once you do this, you can handle any crisis with greater confidence and experience a higher quality of life.

ONE FINAL SUCCESS STRATEGY

You may have heard of visualization, a powerful development tool that uses the power of the mind to help you attain your goals. It involves forming mental images of a desired outcome, and then focusing all your thoughts and efforts towards achieving it. Successful people such as talk show host Oprah Winfrey, actor Arnold Schwarzenegger and ski racer Lindsey Vonn swear by it. Popular actor Will Smith puts it this way:

'In my mind, I've always been an A-list Hollywood superstar. Y'all just didn't know yet.' This technique, when rightly used, can help you attract success, alter your circumstances and make good things happen.

Does this mean that you lie in a hammock and imagine that you are rich, famous, or popular, and it happens just like that? Nope. There are no shortcuts, remember? You first need to visualize the idea in your head and then carry it out through assertive action. This involves having a strong purpose or vision, and then working relentlessly towards it.

If your deepest desire is to become an entrepreneur, for example, you need to take business management classes, intern with successful businessmen, and join groups that will help you build skills and a network of the right people. Maybe your goal is to change from being solitary and inward-looking, into an outgoing person who does not shy away from opportunities. To achieve this, begin by observing people you admire and aspire to be like. Watch how they walk and talk, and how their aura is one of confidence. Start by going to meetings where you feel at home with the topic and have something to offer. If you practise yoga, for instance, join a yoga group where you will find it easy to mingle and voice your opinion.

You can motivate yourself by creating photographs placing you in your ideal situation. For example, if you aspire to run your own travel company, create a collage of pictures with you in front of Big Ben, the Eiffel Tower or Angkor Wat. If your goal is to paint or write your masterpiece, put up a picture of yourself in a hillside cottage where you are free to indulge your muse. As a teenager, we all have our inspirations, rock stars, musicians or sports icons, whose posters we put up on our walls. Where does all that passion go? Rekindle your dreams and tell yourself that you will not let anyone or anything stand in your way! Evoke positive feelings about your goal, take action and keep enforcing your new beliefs and behaviour by making visualization a daily habit.

SOME TIPS ON VISUALIZING SUCCESSFULLY

- Rehearse situations and how you will react to them in your mind until you train your mind to follow this course when the need arises. So, if you want to get a great job, imagine walking confidently into the room, shaking the interviewer's hand firmly and summing up your educational and work-related qualifications. If you want to make a presentation which will make your bosses sit up and take notice, rehearse the whole thing many times and practise answers to different questions that may be asked.
- Use all your senses to picture the scene—the feel of your crisp outfit against your skin, the smell of coffee that fills the room, the surge of confidence as you go flawlessly through each step. Powerful mental images combined with strong emotional responses are excellent motivators, making your subconscious believe that this is really happening.
- Tell yourself each day that you are going to be successful, that you are going to get that promotion, contract, or appreciation. As the Buddha said, 'The mind is everything. What you think, you become.'

Many years back, when I read Robert Kiyosaki's *Rich Dad Poor Dad*, I was impressed by Rich Dad's theory of life. He says that life pushes us around, and some give up easily. Others fight, knowing that success lies in changing ourselves, learning lessons and growing wiser. He also says that our aim should be to escape the rat race, by not working for money but making money work for us. We need to build assets that will generate income. Here are some examples: A business that others run for you, leveraging realty or the stock market, or even royalties. Writing books was the only option I found interesting. And today, I am a full-time author, working towards making a name for myself with my writing!

So, spend some time each day visualizing your goals—whether it is to be respected at home or work—and the joy you will feel when you achieve them.

Once you have chosen your path, work on the change that will come next. Everything depends on you and not on luck or fate. If you wish to change your boring life and go places, stop hanging out at the same places with the same people and instead, look for successful men and women who will inspire you. Ditch the negative souls who suck out your energy, and seek out like-minded people who are generous and encouraging. Do not follow your usual path and expect it to take you to some place new! Ask yourself what will make you happy at this point in your life. Then go ahead and make it happen. Start with something small and experience the new energy coursing through you when you achieve this. Your eyes will be brighter, your steps lighter and your heart happier.

Self-help is a lifelong task, but once you take the first step, it will be easier to take the next. Only you can decide what you need to learn or change to achieve your goals. Maybe, in time, you will become the nucleus around which societal changes will be kick-started. You could inspire others around you to follow your example. Believe in yourself and open yourself up to opportunities and skills that will help you succeed. As the first post-apartheid President of South Africa, Nelson Mandela puts it, 'It always seems impossible until it's done.'

WOMEN HELPING OTHER WOMEN

As women form around 50 per cent of the world's population, we could work together and emerge as a formidable force. It would seem a given that one woman will understand another's difficulties and lend her a helping hand. But unfortunately, we often find that this is not the case. Someone who should applaud your efforts to make a life for yourself is often the one reinforcing society's doubts about your choices or competence. 'It must be true if another woman is saying it!' is the popular opinion. So, you often find that other women mock you when you go out to work. 'Oh, she wants money to spend on clothes and jewellery, and she neglects her husband and children in the process,' they say. The truth may be that your job is necessary for your family's well-being but they are not interested in the facts. They are busy talking about how you will 'pay the price' when your kids go 'astray'.

Why do women not realize that we can all thrive when we help one another? Your neighbour's success does not take away from yours. You do not have to feel guilty or insecure that you did not choose that path. Why not consider it as an option—maybe not for you, but for your sister or your daughter? Together, you can change the world, making choices that are right for you as an individual. Naturally, there can be as many paths as there are women. It is better not to judge other women or try to force-fit them into foolish stereotypes. A stay-at-home mom does not have to keep proving her cooking and housekeeping skills every day. A working woman does not have to be trolled on how she has sacrificed her children's well-being in order to satisfy her ambition. After all, she may already be feeling guilty and stressing herself by trying to do everything for them. Remember, she is doing this in addition to her job. Her responsibilities at home are also waiting for her when she returns.

NOT JUST FOR WOMEN, NOT JUST FOR YOUR OWN GAIN

Speaking up for yourself and for other women inevitably leads to a better world for everyone. You can also expand your horizons by helping the community. Volunteer one evening a week, support a charity, or help a neighbour in need. Your good deed will inspire someone else to do the same and your happiness will multiply. When you stand up for equality and justice, you are initiating a revolution to recreate the world. As the hero of my novel *Pradyumna* puts it, 'We too can lift Mount Govardhana with the power of our minds and win the war that we face every day. This is the time to raise our voices...and our fists if need be.' When men show respect and appreciation towards the women in their lives, they help accelerate change. Note that this cannot be a one-way street and that you need to show your appreciation of men's role as well. Explain to them that you need their support in your quest, and that we need to chip away at flawed societal attitudes to create a world of mutual respect—a world that poet-laureate Rabindranath Tagore visualized in his immortal poem:

> *Where the mind is without fear*
> *and the head is held high...*
> *Into that heaven of freedom,*
> *my Father, let my country awake.*

As we dream of that perfect state, let us look into the story of the perfect woman, the perfect wife—often interpreted as the patient, suffering one—Sita, wife of Rama.

Warrior Sita and the Thousand-headed Ravana

Sita was the ideal woman according to our scriptures. Elders do not tell you to be like Durga or Kali, for they are not human like Sita, nor do they have the familiar appeal that Sita has to the Indian mind. Rama's wife is the ideal for men and women even in the modern world, though she is considered a rather impractical role model in today's environment.

What words would you use to describe Sita? Submissive, suffering, passive? Well, read on and you will find that you may need to rethink this! This story comes from the *Adbhut Ramayana*, where the adjective 'adbhut', or astonishing, indicates that this is not a tale that is told often. The narrator is Valmiki, who tells Sage Bharadvaja that he has composed a hundred crore verses of which only 25,000 are seen in the *Valmiki Ramayana*.

The *Adbhut Ramayana* is the best of the *Ramayana*, he says, as it narrates the glory of Sita that has so far remained hidden. Further, reciting just a single verse from this composition will confer benefits that equal reciting all 25,000 verses of the other version.

Let us learn more about our heroine's adbhut form.

After defeating Dashanan, the ten-headed Ravana in Lanka, Rama returned to Ayodhya with Sita, Lakshmana, Vibhishana and Hanuman, to take back his throne from his brother and establish Rama Rajya. The sages praised his valour and his invincible power and sympathized with Sita who had suffered so much when held captive by Dashanan. Sita laughed on hearing them speak endlessly of her suffering and Rama's bravery. When they looked at her in surprise, she explained that she was amused because she knew of a fiercer rakshasa, Dashanan's twin brother, who had not ten heads but a thousand.

'A sage whom I served faithfully when I was the princess of Mithila told me of Sahasranana Ravana who lives on the island of Pushkar,' she said. 'This rakshasa vanquished Indra and took over his capital, the fabulous Amaravati. A hundred times more powerful than Dashanan, Sahasranana would toss the sun, moon and mountains in the air in sport, as if they were toys. To him, Mount Meru was like a mustard seed and the three worlds like bits of straw. He considered the continents as mere clods of earth and the powerful ocean as a trifling puddle in a cow's footprint. He was ever eager to display his powers, though his father

Vishrava and his grandfather Pulastya entreated him to be humble.'

Angered by Sita's praise of another warrior, Rama vowed that he would battle this rakshasa and kill him just as he had killed Dashanan. 'Accompany me in the Pushpaka Vimana and witness his death!' he told his wife. Sita hesitated for a moment as she was reminded of the time she had been carried off in this very chariot by Dashanan, but then climbed in to sit by Rama's side. The vimana sailed swiftly through the air while Rama's army of men, rakshasas and vanaras followed them over land and water.

Sahasranana's spies brought him news of the foe who was at his gates with an ocean of troops. 'Who is this mortal who courts death so lightly?' he roared.

'He is Rama, King of Ayodhya, who killed your brother Dashanan in Lanka,' pronounced a voice from the heavens.

'I will avenge my brother's death! I will crush this mortal who is so puffed up by conceit that he thinks he can kill me!' said Sahasranana, ordering his rakshasa army to attack the invaders. They charged out of his fortress gates, mounted on horses, elephants and terrifying beasts, setting the earth trembling, their voices raised in challenge. A terrible battle ensued and Rama's army rained havoc on the enemy under the able command of Vibhishana, Sugriva, Hanuman, Rama and his brothers. Seeing his rakshasa troops scatter under the onslaught, Sahasranana came roaring from his palace, his two thousand eyes glittering and his two thousand arms wielding dire weapons. He howled in defiance from his thousand mouths and challenged his foes.

When he laid eyes on the army that confronted him, he decided that they were not worthy enough to fight him. 'How can I demean myself by fighting these feeble humans and animals!' he exclaimed, deciding to get rid of them in another way—sending them back to the lands they hailed from. He sent forth three magical weapons embodying the force of a hundred thousand hurricanes. The men, all except Rama, were hurled back to Ayodhya. Vibhishana and his rakshasa troops were propelled through space to Lanka, and the vanaras, including Hanuman, to the forests of Kishkinda.

'I need no army to kill you. I challenge you to single combat!' declared a furious Rama, charging towards his enemy, inundating him with fierce arrows from his bow, Kodanda. But Sahasranana took a thousand forms, each armed with fearsome weapons, and deflected Rama's attack with his monstrous shields. Rama saw through the illusion and brought out the invincible arrow he had used to kill Dashanan. He sent it thundering through the air at the real Ravana, but his foe laughed mockingly as he grabbed the arrow in mid-flight and broke it over his knee.

Indra feared that Rama would be defeated and that the rakshasa would then turn his ire on him. 'I pray for your victory, Rama,' he said, 'but you must have realized that Sahasranana Ravana cannot be defeated. Once, in a playful mood, he even plunged mighty Vishnu on his

Garuda, into the deep sea.'

The devas were getting ready to flee from Pushkar, but Sita remained calm and unflinching by her husband's side. The fight continued fiercely through day and night, with magical javelins and occult chakras clashing with uncanny force. Rama grew tired as he was unable to bring down his formidable foe. Ravana then took advantage of his weakness to pierce him with a potent arrow that first passed through Rama's body and then through earth to enter the netherworld. Rama fell to the earth from the vimana, and swooned from the horrific pain.

Sahasranana pounded his chest in triumph, while the devas and sages berated Sita for telling Rama about this rakshasa. 'The battle that Rama fought and won in Lanka has been rendered meaningless by his current defeat! Look how he lies, as if he were dead,' they lamented.

Sita was provoked by their words and distraught on seeing her beloved Rama lying motionless. She erupted in rage, transforming herself into a terrifying goddess with four arms and a huge body adorned with garlands of skulls and anklets of bones. Her unbound hair flowed down her back like a torrent and her eyes rolled in frenzy. In her hands, she held awful weapons including a bell and a noose signifying the destruction of life. Her fanged mouth opened wide as if to swallow all creation and she charged forward on the back of a lion to engage the demons in a savage battle. She tore off their heads with her talons and wore their entrails as garlands. Then she turned on Ravana. She slashed off his thousand heads with one swift stroke of her glittering sword and began to toss the heads in the air as if they were balls for her to play with. From her body sprang a thousand Matrikas, fierce demonesses that slaughtered the rakshasas and drank their blood.

The Devi's roars splintered the skies. The earth shuddered and began to sink into the netherworld. The sages were terrified and prostrated themselves before her. 'Have mercy on us, divine Mother!' they prayed. 'Preserve the three realms that are threatened by your incandescent rage.'

Sita was still angry and her fierce breath burned the heavens. Brahma appeared before her and joined his hands in worship. 'Desist from your fury, Great Goddess!' he said. 'Tell us what we must do to placate you.'

The Devi motioned to Rama, who was lying lifeless on the ground. 'How can I soften my rage when my Rama lies unmoving before me?' she replied, her eyes shooting fire.

Brahma revived Rama by sprinkling sacred water on him and the warrior rose swiftly to his feet. He stared awestruck at the fierce, many-armed figure looming over him and looked fearfully at the devastation that she had wreaked. Brahma explained what had happened when Rama had been unconscious. 'Sahasranana has been killed by Devi Bhadrakali, who is none other than your own Sita,' he said. 'She is Shakti, she is Nature. Sita embodies the cosmic power that creates, preserves and destroys the universe. She is the gentle Gauri, the fierce Durga and the dreaded Kali. No god can act without her blessing. Sita is no less than you, Rama, for she is both Prakriti, the creative power of the universe, and Purusha, the consciousness within.'

The Devi granted Rama divine sight so that he could see her in her omnipotent form of Parameshwari, just as Krishna would show his Vishvarupa to Arjuna in a later age. She revealed to him the wisdom of the *Gita* that is foreshadowed in the *Adbhut Ramayana*, where Valmiki substitutes Shakti for Krishna in a famous verse: 'Whenever dharma declines, Prakriti appears on earth to destroy adharma'.

Rama praised the divine goddess, reciting the 'Kali Sahasranama'—her thousand names. He was moved to tears to see her secret form and true greatness. He realized now that his wife was no helpless maiden but a potent goddess who could have severed Dashanan's sister Surpanakha's nose herself and burned Dashanan to ashes if she had so wished. She had chosen, instead, to allow herself to be abducted so that Rama could kill Ravana and re-establish righteousness on earth. His Sita had restrained herself so his own power as husband and king would not be diminished. Now, however, she had revealed her potency in order to save Rama from a far greater danger.

The gods worshipped the Devi by whose grace the divine plan was now complete. They realized that they could prosper only through Adi Shakti's blessings. They eulogized her as the beginning of creation and the cause of all actions. They praised her as the abode of the great Kundalini that energizes the moving and unmoving universe. They hailed Sita as the force behind the killing of both Ravanas. The goddess displayed her inner fierceness when it was needed, just as Rama had done to destroy demons.

The splendorous Devi revealed to Rama that she resided inside all human beings in the same form that she had assumed to kill Sahasranana. She was both human and divine—just as mortals are. It was her human form that was subjected to suffering but her essence remained potent and untouched. Then, she offered Rama a boon and he asked that her divine form remain always in his heart. She smiled and nodded.

'Return, Great Goddess, to your human form, as my eyes are dazzled,' he requested her, and she resumed her gentle form of Sita. The two returned to Ayodhya to continue their divine reign.

SMILE LIKE SITA, FOR YOU TOO HAVE THE POWER

Are you surprised to meet this Sita, who is not at all like the ever suffering wife you see in the *Valmiki Ramayana*? Her abduction and travails occupy just one section of the total twenty-seven in the *Adbhut Ramayana*, and she smiles throughout the book, like the goddess you see in the temple. It is Rama who cries at being separated from her, with his tears creating the river Vaitarani, and filling up the diminished ocean. You see Sita portrayed as Adi Shakti and Vaishnava

Shakti, before whom Rama's power wanes. When her inner Durga is aroused, she kills a mighty foe and rescues her husband. What a reversal of roles! No wonder then that this version is not commonly known, as her character does not fit into the gender stereotypes imposed by a patriarchal society.

This Sita delivers a warning to the world, of the consequences of dishonouring women, remaining recognizable as Sita even when she takes the Kali form. Through this marvellous tale, you are able to understand that a goddess can take on many forms but still retain her identity. Many of the Matrikas or mother goddesses who emerge from the Devi, bear names commonly used by Indian women, such as Prabha, Madhavi, Kamala and Jaya. This indicates that the goddess within you can be aroused at any time to recreate your world and your relationships. When Sita is found in a furrow by King Janaka, a heavenly voice tells him that this child will promote the welfare of all life. Like her, you too can be the benevolent Lakshmi who sits calmly by Vishnu's side or the dire Kali who embodies true feminine power.

LESSONS LEARNED

Free yourself to emulate Sita, though not the long-suffering one you see in movies or books. Remember that even the gentle Sita of Valmiki rebels when forced to walk through the fire a second time to prove her chastity. She defies misogynists who cast aspersions on her character. Her power is such that even the Fire God dare not touch or harm her. Her sense of right and wrong is superior to Rama's, the most perfect of men. She refuses to forsake dharma even when her husband forgets his duty to protect her. Ultimately, she becomes the eternal symbol of strength, dignity and divinity. 'Jai Siya Ram!' is the universal chant, where her name precedes Rama's, for he is incomplete without her.

Sita can inspire you to assert your moral strength when society makes unreasonable demands. Like her, you also undergo trials by fire in your life. But you will pass through these unharmed, when you reject the mean minds that torment you, and break the bars that seek to confine you. You are not born to weep—no woman is. Remember that you are not living in the Victorian Age when it was believed that 'men must work and women must weep!' Visualize the smile of the goddess that radiates bliss and benevolence. Allow the power within you to demolish hurdles you face. Like the Devi who transforms ignorance to knowledge, and bondage to liberation, you too can evolve from weakness to strength, from submissiveness to power. Just speak up and watch your life change.

Conclusion:
Creating a New Shakti—You!

Pat yourself on the back! You have come this far, showing that you are truly invested in changing your personality and, thereby, your life. You may have identified the problem that holds you back, which in itself is a great beginning. The next step that you may have started implementing already, is to initiate changes in order to make your life more meaningful and rewarding. You have seen what makes change so difficult—the many ways in which family, society or your own mind act to obstruct your path. The three Cs—Choose, Change and Create—will give you an easy-to-remember strategic plan to apply to each facet of your life. You have met several women in this book who face difficult situations just like you. You will be able to identify with their struggles and get a better perspective when you see where they are going wrong. It's always easier to see the wrong choices that others make, rather than your own.

Realizing what needs to be changed makes it easy to use the three Cs to improve your life. This step-by-step guide will help you achieve your desire and also prepare you to face others' reactions to your new persona. Finally, you will internalize your rights as a wife, mother, an employee or daughter, making key decisions regarding marriage or career. You will also profit from the many tips given in the book to deal with difficult family members, bosses and society at large.

Start implementing these ideas at once if you have not done so already. These lessons are born of experience and observation over a long period of time during which people's behaviour has changed, but not with regard to women's issues. The steps are practical, easy to follow and begin to show results almost at once. You may think that your problem is insurmountable or that it's too late to make a change now. You may feel that you are hampered emotionally, physically or financially and that you are unlikely to succeed.

However, it is important for you to know that your goals are reachable and that YOU can reach them. You can take small steps forward, make the necessary changes at a pace that suits you, and reach your final objective. Each small victory and the joy it brings will help you imagine what you will feel when you reach your destination, motivating you to continue your course. Remember that some steps may take you longer than others and that it is okay to fail sometimes. Life has a way of interfering and difficult people or circumstances keep cropping up. You may be forced to climb over hurdles, move them aside or avoid them altogether. If you have made a mistake, no worries. Be kind to yourself and pick up from where you left off. Don't dwell on your mistakes or on the wrongs that others have done to you. This will only slow you down and make you feel that you are going to fail, no matter how hard you try. What you do today, how you move forward again and the momentum you build up are what matter. You need to make the right choice here, as these choices will define who you are and how far you will progress. Start the process immediately so that you can experience the benefits at the earliest.

ESCAPE STEREOTYPES

Remember that self-empowerment is what you define it to be. It's the confidence you build to act and speak for yourself, and to realize that you can be anything and everything you want to be. Earlier generations regarded women as 'property', and were obsessed with confining her within four walls to preserve her 'purity'. Interpretations of our mythology also focused on her chastity and devotion to her husband, disregarding all her other qualities and accomplishments. Many crimes are still committed in the name of 'honour', for a woman is regarded not as an individual with rights, but as an embodiment of her family's and community's dignity. Gradually, women have begun speaking up against these ideas and asking sharp questions.

For instance, why are there no role models for men, who display total fidelity and love? Even the ideal man, Rama, prioritizes his people over his wife. These days, popular opinion exhibited in movies and media represents a 'liberated' woman as one who is strident, who smokes and drinks and wears short skirts. Do not get trapped in this stereotype after escaping the one of the passive, submissive woman. You do not have to follow the path of other women even if they assert that only *their* choices are 'cool'. Show the world that you are confident of yourself, of walking boldly into any situation and coming out unharmed. You are not competing with others or judging them. You are no longer afraid of what life may throw at you.

Move steadily towards this ideal, knowing that you need to merely tap into your unlimited potential and dormant abilities. Do not worry about the results, for once you begin acting, results will automatically follow. Take responsibility for yourself, make the changes that will make you happier, healthier and more successful. The first time you assert yourself may be difficult, but it gets easier with each successive attempt, until it becomes second nature. It frees up your mind and time and you begin to wonder why you hadn't done this all these years. Never mind! You've started now and that's all that matters. Discover your dream and work towards making it real, whether you are twenty, forty or sixty years of age. Prove to yourself that you have the guts to do what you want and then enjoy the glory. Learn to handle the reactions from others when they find that you have changed, that you now have a voice and are not afraid to use it. Tap into the universal energy of other women who are no longer hiding their light but living their lives with pride. There could be no better time than now, when each day we see more women speaking up—against abuse, against oppression, against victimization.

CHERISH THE TRUE 'YOU'

Being assertive does not mean that you should shun the so-called feminine facets of your personality or the simpler pleasures of life. If you force yourself to do this, you will be swamped by a sense of dissatisfaction that could lead to illness, depression or even a breakdown.

Enjoy a sunset, inhale the scent of freshly brewed coffee, cuddle your pet, feed the birds and watch them trill with delight. Clear out the clutter and surround yourself with the beauty of flowers, plants, paintings or music. Wear flowing skirts, chunky bracelets, glossy lip colours—anything that engages your senses and uplifts your spirit. Make time for yourself by asking family, friends or professionals for help when needed. Remember that a happier 'you' will make them happier too.

Love your body and treat it with respect. Forget the trolls who criticize your shape or size. Get rid of toxic relationships and patterns that stifle your growth. Meditate, pray, offer flowers to a deity—do whatever brings you peace. Shine as you were meant to shine, so that you can inspire other women and enable men to see you for what you are. Balancing your focused and forceful side with your soft and caring side will bring you greater joy—at home and at work.

LIBERATE THE GODDESS IN YOU

Finally, tune into the powers of the goddesses revealed in the stories that I have extracted from our puranas. Society has kept these inspiring stories largely hidden, in a bid to keep women from realizing their strengths or knowing that they are in no way inferior to men. Women who have been suppressed and manipulated and lack control over their own destinies, can seek inspiration and healing through these goddesses. Like

RUPA
5174 6-10-18

them, you too can battle hostile forces and emerge stronger, with new hope and faith that are the foundations of great religions. Amba, the mother goddess, calls her daughters to fight alongside her, to carry forward the fight against gender bias and create a more equitable world. Her force enables you to transcend your own fears or societal constraints to enter a brighter, higher plane. Tap into Lakshmi's power of abundance, Durga's fierce energy and Saraswati's gift of wisdom. Durga is particularly potent, as she unites the 'fierce' with the 'protective', and the masculine with the feminine, in a marriage of equals. Like her, you too can be mother, wife or torchbearer for equality, choosing the right path to take you to your goal.

FROM ME TO YOU

I hope that this book will help you find freedom and fulfilment in your personal and professional life. I look forward to a day when you will become an inspiration for others to create change. I wish that more men join women in this struggle to break barriers. Share your story with me, and get in touch through my website or social media. We need to speak up, look for solutions, believe in ourselves and reach farther every day. I send you healing and positive vibes so that you may find and unleash the power within you.

Enjoy each day of the new, empowered 'you'. Be happy, be YOU.